Origin of a Vendetta

"Hey—Dan," George said, and blood spurted from his mouth in a fine spray as he coughed. Dan Track cradled his nephew in his arm, a Magnum clenched in his fist. "Dan... I told mom you'd come to bail us out. How...."

George's voice faltered, and for a moment Track couldn't speak. George's mother had been dead for ten years. A shiver raced along Track's spine, and his vision suddenly blurred. When it came, his voice was tight and strained. "She's... she's fine, George. She's fine."

"I told her you'd come," George said, his voice a whisper. And then George's head rolled back. For a moment, Track couldn't see whether his nephew's chest still rose, or tell if the pulse in his neck still throbbed.

"George!" Track screamed, trying to call the young man back from the dead.

But George's chest still did not rise, and Track hung his head over his nephew's face and wept.

Now available in the exciting new series from Gold Eagle Books

TRACK

by Jerry Ahern

#1 The Ninety-Nine
#2 Atrocity
#3 The Armageddon Conspiracy
#4 The Hard Way
#5 Origin of a Vendetta

TRACK

Origin of a Vendetta

JERRY AHERN

A GOLD EAGLE BOOK FROM
WORLDWIDE

TORONTO • NEW YORK • LONDON • PARIS
AMSTERDAM • STOCKHOLM • HAMBURG
ATHENS • MILAN • TOKYO • SYDNEY

To the readers who wanted to see Track,
Desiree and Zulu together again—
here they are. All the best....

First edition February 1985

ISBN 0-373-62005-5

Printed in Canada

1

The sun seemed incredibly bright to him, and already heat rose in shimmering yellow waves as Dan Track adjusted his sunglasses and began to peel his brown leather bomber jacket from his back. Morning on the desert had been cold, but now Track's blue cowboy shirt was dark with sweat, and the leather of the shoulder harness housing the Smith & Wesson .357 stained and uncomfortable. Track squinted across the rise. Ahead of him, George Beegh had assumed a rifleman's prone position on the lip that overlooked the valley beyond. George's rifle lay on the bleached rocks beside him, while he scanned the valley with his binoculars. As Dan Track watched his nephew, the younger man slung the 8x30s over his left shoulder, picked up his Aimpoint-sighted M-16 and edged back on knees and elbows.

Track set his bomber jacket on the sandy ground beside a lightning-struck pine stump, and took up the matte-black shape of his SPAS-12 in both fists. Working the magazine cutoff, he took a solitary red plastic high-brass Federal 2 3/4-inch double-0 buck load from the watchpocket of his Levi's and inserted it into the SPAS's chamber. Track set both safeties and let the bolt slide forward. With eight double-0 bucks up the magazine tube, plus the one he had just loaded into the chamber, the SPAS was ready. He set the SPAS beside the stump and picked up an M-16. He checked the seating of the 30-round magazine, eared back the bolt and let it fly forward to strip and chamber the top round, then set the safety. As he removed the rubber lens covers from the potentiameter-fitted Aimpoint and stuffed them into his right breast pocket, George stood in front of him.

"They're all down there," George murmured, lighting a Winston with a disposable lighter. "It's all right." George nodded, answering an unasked question. "Wind's blowing away from the valley—they won't see the smoke."

Dan Track nodded, taking a Cuesta-Rey Six-T from his bomber jacket. He guillotined the thin, dark cigar's tip, fired it in the blue-yellow flame of his Zippo and inhaled the smoke deep into his lungs. "How many, George?"

"Men or airplanes?"

Track shrugged. "Tell me the good news first—how many airplanes?"

"I stopped counting at twenty-five, but there's at least half as many more. They're so packed in down there that only one could take off or land at a time."

"Now the bad news—how many men?"

"Little more than a dozen men, with two Jeeps, a van, a Toyota Land Cruiser that looks like it was the target in a hammer-throwing contest and a Trans Am muscle car—carburetor's up higher than the hood. I'd go cross-eyed driving one of those."

Track let himself smile. "Twelve guys or so?"

"About that."

Track shrugged. "Well, don't worry. You pick the guys you want, and I'll take the one or two you don't. Pass me the binocs—and be careful with these things." Track grinned, taking them from George's hand. "They cost money, you know?" Track set his M-16 beside the SPAS. "And don't step on my coat," Track added, smiling as he walked toward the lip of the rise, George mimicking him in a low whisper. After he'd gone about twenty feet, Track dropped to his hands and knees and crawled forward to avoid silhouetting himself on the rise. A slight breeze kicked up, and the sand attacked his skin like a thousand needles as sweat streamed down his face. He reminded himself to wear a hat the next time he was in the desert. He glanced back at George; a black Jack Daniels baseball cap was pulled low over his nephew's eyes.

Then Dan Track put the binoculars to his eyes and looked over the rise, the dual-focus rings moving under his fingertips as he sharpened the image to study the valley floor. A Lear jet and a Duke V-60 caught his eye.

He panned away from the stolen planes, along the valley floor. "Shit," Track rasped. George had neglected to mention that each of the Jeeps had an M-60 mounted in the back. But then again, he thought, no one manned the Jeeps at the moment, or the guns. He tightened his focus. One of the Jeeps had ammo cans nestled near the machine gun. "Hmm," Track murmured. "Possibilities." Most of the men of the aircraft theft ring lounged under improvised shelters or beneath the wings of the stolen aircraft, trying to escape the midmorning heat. Two stood guard at the far edge of the valley, where a niche in the rocks allowed a rough ranch road to cut through.

Dan Track swung the binoculars to his right. At the eastern edge of the landing field he could see the parked van—it was camouflage painted, but very poorly. Four men stood in its shadow, and like the guards flanking the road, each carried a restricted weapon—either an AR-15 or an M-16. At the distance it was impossible to tell. Violating federal firearms laws, specifically the "Gangster Weapons" act of 1935, probably wouldn't bother men who had stolen more than one hundred private and business aircraft in the last eighteen months. Track glanced at the black-faced Rolex Sea-Dweller on his left wrist. Twenty minutes earlier, he had radioed to Sir Abner Chesterton, his liaison with the Consortium of International Insurance Underwriters for whom Track worked, suggesting that Sir Abner contact the Texas Rangers. It would be another fifteen minutes at the inside before the Texas Department of Public Safety helicopters arrived.

Track swallowed hard—the men in the valley were beginning to stir. "Oh, shit," he snarled. He looked behind him and made a low whistle. George turned, catching the signal, and came in a low run, his rifle at high port. As Track peered down into the valley he heard the shuffling sound of sand and gravel as George dropped to his knees beside him.

"What's up, Uncle Dan? Aww, great—" George muttered as he looked over the rise.

Track looked at his nephew, saying nothing.

"They're moving. Wonderful—the Rangers'll never get here in time."

"Right," Track replied. "So we gotta grab one of those Jeeps with an M-60 on board—otherwise, we got problems. They'll either get away or we'll try and bust them and they'll kill us and get away anyway."

"You got the high ground," George said. "You're the better marksman—give me the SPAS and you keep both M-16s."

"You should have brought the MPK, George. . ." Track began.

"How the hell was I supposed to know we'd get

into a firefight and need that Walther squirt gun—shit, Dan!"

"Anyway, that's a good plan—I'll cover you from up here, start shooting when you get down there," Track said, pointing to a spot near the valley floor. "Then we play it by ear. Try not to damage any of the airplanes—Sir Abner's gonna have to answer to the Consortium for every bullet hole."

"Yeah, well so long as the holes aren't in us."

Track nodded. "Clean the shells out of my jacket. Leave me eight buckshot just in case. You take the rest. There's a couple of slug loads in there." Track looked at his nephew. "Hey—be careful, huh?"

"You just feel that way because I'm lovable, Uncle Dan. It's those puppy-dog eyes I've got, that's what melts everybody's heart."

"Right," Track said as he nodded. "Why don't you leave the SPAS here and go down there weaponless and let *them* see your puppy-dog eyes—get them to surrender without firing a shot."

"Bite it, Dan," George laughed as he started to edge back from the lip of the rise, leaving his M-16 in the dirt beside Track. Track scanned the valley floor, then let the binoculars drop on their black vinyl neckstrap and started edging back himself. He stopped after a few feet and watched for a moment as George picked up the SPAS-12. George made a thumbs-up signal and gestured toward the

FIE shotgun. Track held up eight fingers, then one. George nodded; he understood. Then he slung the SPAS over his shoulder and started to search Track's bomber jacket for the spare rounds for the police shotgun.

Track looked at George a moment longer. George was the son of Track's dead elder sister, Diane. George had his mother's eyes, his mother's bizarre sense of humor. Track found himself smiling, remembering the woman, really only a girl, who had raised him, their parents dead—tragically, violently, unalterably. Track turned away from George, suddenly bringing the binoculars up to his eyes to stare down into the valley. The men were loading gear aboard their vehicles, but still the two Jeeps with the M-60s were unmanned. Track squinted his eyes, barely able to see for an instant. He hadn't thought of the death of his mother and father, and then the death of his sister and her husband, Robert Beegh, for a very long time.

He turned around to call to George not to go down into the valley—but George was gone.

All the others that he cared for were dead. Except for George. The death of George's mother had been a hard thing for the boy, and Track had not discussed it with George for years.

Track stared back into the valley. For the fact that Robert Beegh had given him a home of sorts, he supposed he was grateful. And he was sorry for

Robert's death. But he had never liked the man. His memory of Robert Beegh was of a man who was rarely home, made little money and almost never sent any of it back to his young wife and her baby. "Shit," Track said, sniffing loudly. He had dropped out of high school for many reasons, but one of them had been to ease Diane's financial burden in caring for George. Dan Track had never told his nephew that.

He refocused the binoculars—maybe that would help, he thought... but it didn't help at all.

GEORGE BEEGH CROUCHED just behind the rock-cut through which the ranch road ran, leading into the valley. The pistol grip of the SPAS-12 was clamped in his right fist, the shotgun tensioned against its sling away from his body. The action was set to fire on semiautomatic rather than pump, as his uncle had left it. Only the quick employment safety was on, his right index finger ever so slightly edged against it to nudge it forward, ready to snap back against the trigger.

Both palms sweated.

George pulled the Jack Daniels baseball cap lower over his eyes and started down from the lowest of the rocks, keeping to the far edge of the road. There were sounds of automobile engines firing, but no sounds of gunfire, no shouts of panic, no curses of threatened reprisal.

He wanted a cigarette—badly. George felt a

smile cross his lips. He always acted annoyed when his uncle told him that he should quit smoking, but he was happy that his uncle cared. As George kept moving, he reflected that his memories of Dan Track were an odd assortment. He remembered Dan Track in some ways vaguely, in other ways very vividly. It was Dan who had taught him how to ride a two-wheeled bicycle. George remembered the gleaming chrome, and he remembered too asking Dan where he'd gotten the money for the bike and that Dan had never told him. The bike had been fully assembled and brand-new.... "Naw," he murmured under his breath. The two guards were in sight, M-16s held more at the ready than they had been. George kept moving.

For some reason, he remembered the bike a lot. Once it was stolen and he had cried, and Dan had said something to George's mother. The next morning, the bike was back in his bedroom and his uncle's face bruised and his forearm bandaged. He'd known his uncle well enough to know Dan Track had found the people who stole the bike and had stolen it back from them.

And he remembered Dan Track going away to join the Army, after just coming back from being "away" for two weeks. He'd since realized his uncle had been in a juvenile hall awaiting a hearing. There had been no money for bail, no money for a lawyer. Dan had dropped to his knees and held

George in his arms and told him, "Whatever you hear them say about me on the street, well—I didn't have anything to do with killing that guy. I did a lot of things maybe I shouldn't have, but I didn't have anything to do with killing that guy." His uncle had held him close.

Every month there had been a check, as regular as clockwork, and there was always food on the table. And then his father had come back and they had moved. His father threw away the bicycle and Dan stopped writing letters and sending postcards and presents from Germany. And George's mother began crying a lot again.

The years before his parents had been killed in the automobile accident had been confusing years. He knew his father was some kind of scientist but had never understood what kind. After they had died, the FBI agents had come to ask him questions and Dan—he was a captain by then—had told them to leave George alone. And George had gone to Germany with his uncle and lived with him six months before entering a military academy. Then it had been the Air Force, even though his uncle had promised to pay his way through college. He hadn't wanted that. His uncle had done enough.

He remembered the only time Dan had returned before his parents had died. His mother had taken a photograph—the three men she loved, she had said. That night he heard his father and his uncle arguing, and the next morning Dan was gone and his mother was crying again.

He shook himself free of his memories. He was close to the guards now, almost close enough to smell their sweat. He looked to the lip of the rise, but saw nothing—his uncle was too good to be seen.

George swung his SPAS-12 forward on its sling, working off the quick deployment safety.

Cold blood wasn't something he could quite handle and he was glad of it.

"Freeze, sucker!" he shouted.

What he knew would happen, happened. The nearest of the two men wheeled around, his M-16 coming on line. George's trigger finger twitched and the guard's body slammed back into the second guard even as the other man's left temple spotted red with blood. Double-0 buck made a mess wherever it went.

George heard the sharp crack of an M-16 on semiauto from the rise.

Jumping both bodies, he raced through the rock-cut, toward the nearest of the two Jeeps and its M-60 machine gun. The staccato rhythm of gunfire beat the air, and men were dying all around him. The SPAS thundered in his hands and the sharp cracks of assault-rifle fire in neat 3-round bursts exploded from the rise.

George reached the nearest of the two Jeeps, jumped aboard and seized one of the ammo cans he'd seen from above. Bullets zinged off the metal of the Jeep. George exhaled loudly in a sigh of relief—the 7.62mm NATO ball ammo was already packed in push-through links. George laid the SPAS on the bed of the Jeep and hauled at the visible end of the ammo belt, slinging it over his shoulder. He shifted the M-60's safety into the fire position, drawing back the bolt with his right hand until the cocking lever clicked into its full rearward position. He eased the cocking lever forward to engage the retaining latch, then reset the safety. Raising the latch cover, he placed the link belt onto the feed plate, then hit the deck as a fusilade of automatic-weapons fire pounded into the Jeep.

A solitary man charged the Jeep with an M-16. George pulled the Smith 469 from his shoulder rig, working the safety, double-actioning the first shot. The man shuddered as George kept working on the trigger, until the body gyrated into the sand in a spastic dance of death. More assault-rifle fire plowed into the sand of the valley from the rise. He had the first round in the feed-plate groove, reciting the litany of operation to himself, checking that the links were up and that the feed plate engaged the second round as well. Then George slammed the cover down, latching it.

His right thumb found the safety again, pushing the lever forward and up. George swung the M-60 on its tripod, working the trigger in and out, the low cyclic rate easy to control in 3-round bursts.

Firing again and again, he cut into the enemy forces that had formed a wedge between the Jeep and the single runway. Men started to run toward the vehicles, and the camouflaged van was approaching from the far end of the valley, men leaning out the open side doors, firing M-16s. George swung the M-60 toward them, burst-firing at the van's front end. The windshield shattered, and the van careened away from him. He saw one of the gunners at the side door hurtling free of the van, rolling. George swung the M-60 toward the man, but the man's rifle was already shouldered. As George pulled the trigger of the machine gun, he felt something tear at him, slamming his body back. The muzzle of the M-60 rocked upward as his hand fell away from the pistol grip. He was on fire with pain. "Jesus," he screamed. His right hand clasped his abdomen and he looked down—sticky red blood oozed through his fingers. Another burst of assault-rifle fire smashed into his flesh. His body was lifted up with the force of the impact, and his insides burned as he rolled, falling, his mouth suddenly filled with sand. He was choking, gagging. Blood mixing with his spittle.

He was afraid to move his right hand. He had heard of men holding their guts in with their hands. He reached behind him with his left, awkwardly freeing the Colt Combat Government .45 from its waistband holster. Suddenly he saw his mother's face and he shouted, "Mom! Get outa here! Mom! You'll get yourself killed, mom!" He stabbed the .45 forward in his left hand, awkwardly getting his thumb to down the safety, firing at a man climbing up into the Jeep to get to the M-60. "Eat lead, son of a bitch!" he screamed. And then he saw his mother again. They were shooting at his mom, he realized. He pushed himself to his knees, then staggered to his feet, firing the .45 from his left fist, firing it until it was empty, downing two more men trying to kill his mom. "Mom! I'm coming, mom! Mom!" Another man raced up to George, the butt of his M-16 raised to strike. George slammed the pistol across the man's forehead and fell against the muzzle of the rifle as the M-16 discharged. George's nerves were seared again and then his legs buckled under him. "Mom! Dan'll save you, mom!" George closed his eyes—just for a second, he told himself....

DAN TRACK SKIDDED DOWN the sandy side of the valley wall on his heels and his rear end, trying to keep both M-16s firing as bursts of assault-rifle fire tore up the ground on both sides of him. Suddenly he screamed, and the M-16 flew out of his left fist. A rifleman's bullet had plowed a furrow into his left forearm, tearing muscle and tendon.

He rolled down the slope, oblivious to the gunfire pouring toward him. The M-16 in his right fist was empty and he let it drop. His right hand found the butt of his Trapper Scorpion, and Track brought it up firing, downing the man nearest him. Track fired two more head shots, just to be sure. Upping the ambidextrous safety, he shoved the pistol into his trouser belt. His right fist grabbed the M-16 from the sand, and he stabbed the rifle ahead of him like a sword, firing what was left of the magazine, downing two more of the aircraft thieves.

Stumbling, he threw the gun into the face of another man. Pulling out the Scorpion, he emptied the last two rounds from the magazine into the man's face. Track's left arm hung dead at his side. The action opened, he jammed the Scorpion into his belt and snatched the S&W .357 L-Frame from the shoulder rig under his left arm. He could see his left forearm—the wetness of sweat had been replaced with the slick darkness of blood.

Track double-actioned the L-Frame, killing another man with a shot into the neck. Blood erupted from torn arteries.

Track sank to his knees and lurched forward as a wave of pain and nausea washed over him. As he rolled onto his back, he double-actioned the Metalife Custom L-Frame again—a head shot, the man's hands flying to cover his eyes as he spread-eagled into the sand.

Track rolled onto his belly and crawled forward on his knees.

He saw George sprawled ten yards from the Jeep, the sand dark and wet around George's abdomen and back. George was still and silent.

Against the side of the Jeep, he pushed himself to his feet.

Track winced as he pulled himself into the Jeep. A white-hot spear of pain pierced his spine, and his head and chest felt as though they were clamped in the jaws of a vise. He felt cold, and he realized that he had a bleeder and he might go unconscious at any moment.

Track leaned forward, vomiting, the meager breakfast he'd eaten before going into the desert pouring from his mouth. He stumbled, letting the .357 drop from his fingers.

His right fist closed on the pistol grip of the M-60 mounted on the Jeep, and his index finger found the trigger and squeezed. Men went down screaming before the flash of muzzle. Heat shimmered off the barrel as Track sprayed out wave after wave of lead. He realized he was burning out the barrel. "Sue me, assholes!" He screamed the words, firing over and over, his finger still moving long after the gun was silent.

There was no one stirring.

He squinted his eyes against the sun, a blistering fireball in the desert sky. Sweat flowed freely down his face from his forehead and his hair. He tried desperately not to surrender to the pain and nausea. He had to get to George.

Using the M-60 to brace his body, he pushed himself to his feet, weaving, his head suddenly light. He stumbled over the side of the Jeep, landing hard in the sand, screaming as pain ripped along his left forearm with jagged teeth.

"George!" He shouted the name, his mouth tasting foul from his own vomit.

He reached out and his fingers closed around the .357 Magnum.

He fell forward on his face when he tried to stand, and he started to crawl toward his nephew.

Sand filled his mouth as he inched forward.

"George!" Track coughed the name, spitting out sand. His mouth was dry and his lips swollen.

George's head moved, and Track lurched forward. He dragged himself beside the younger man and lifted George's head off the sand and rested it on his leg. Blood trickled from George's mouth.

George's eyes opened, and Track saw they were unfocused.

"Hey—Dan," George said, and blood spurted in a fine spray as he coughed. Dan Track cradled his nephew in his good arm, the Magnum clenched in his fist to protect him. "Dan...I told mom you'd come and bail us out. How—"

George's voice faltered, and for a moment Track couldn't speak. George's mother had been dead for a long time. A shiver raced along his spine, and his vision suddenly blurred. When it came, his voice was tight and strained. "She's...she's fine, George. She's fine."

"I—I told her you'd come...you'd...you'd come for—"

And George's head rolled back. For a moment Dan Track couldn't see if his nephew's chest still rose, or tell if the pulse in his neck still throbbed.

"George!" Track screamed the name. He started to scream the younger man's name again, trying to call him back from the dead, but the air suddenly filled with the thunder of helicopters and then a voice boomed over a bullhorn.

"Drop your weapons! Texas Rangers—you are under arrest!"

Dan Track's throat felt raw as he screamed George's name again. But his nephew's chest still did not rise, and Track hung his head over George's face and wept.

2

Dan Track looked at the woman standing over him. He cleared his throat and it ached. When he started to talk his voice sounded odd to him. "Get Sir Abner, Sir Abner Chesterton—get him." Track turned his head—his neck was stiff. He looked to his right, through the venetian blinds at the dying light. He couldn't move his left arm, and every time he tried, spasms of pain shrieked up his arm and hammered against his brain. He vaguely remembered the Texas Rangers, and seeing George carried off on a stretcher, the stretcher lashed to the skid of the largest of the three helicopters.

He remembered waking up with an IV tube in him—someone had said it was blood and he'd passed out again when they'd given him another shot.

He heard the door open but didn't look.

"How is he?" Track asked.

The voice that came back was well modulated, very British. "We don't quite know. There's a bullet fragment lodged near the heart—they're operating now."

"Get me outside the operating room—now!"

"But Dan, you've lost so much blood and—"

"Does one of the member companies insure this place?"

"Dan, you—"

Track turned his head—too fast, pain again—and stared at Sir Abner Chesterton. "Does the Consortium insure this hospital?"

"Yes—"

"Tell them unless they get a wheelchair in here for me and move me outside the damn operating room, you pull their coverage, all of it—understand?"

"I understand more than you might realize in your current state, but I'll do it." Sir Abner Chesterton left the room and the door swung shut behind him.

Dan Track stared at the doorway, willing it to open that much more quickly. Finally, Chesterton returned, followed by a nurse pushing a wheelchair. "This is against all hospital policy," she intoned religiously. "And Mr. Chesterton indicated—"

"Just get me in the chair, sweetheart," Track urged.

Track looked at the IV tube in his right hand. "What—sugar water?"

"It's to. . ." the nurse began.

"I know what it's to—" And Track tore the needle from his hand. Blood oozed from beneath the bandage.

"You can't—" The nurse protested.

"I say, Dan—" Chesterton muttered weakly.

Track stared them down. "Get me into the chair, and get me outside the operating room. Now!" It was his most menacing tone.

The pain of moving was excruciating and he forced his mind to concentrate on something else.

He swung into the chair, sagging back, looking into the nurse's eyes. "Look, I'm sorry—but the boy in the operating room, he's, ahh—"

Track heard Chesterton's voice from behind him. "He's Major Track's nephew. The major has known the young man since he was an infant. They're more than friends—more like father and son. And Major Track holds himself responsible for Mr. Beegh's injuries in combat." Track stared at Chesterton's eyes for a moment and wondered for whose benefit the Englishman had said that. Chesterton almost whispered, his face seamed with a smile, "I supposed the truth might be best for all of us, Daniel."

Track nodded. "Give me a cigarette," he demanded. Chesterton rarely smoked, but always carried cigarettes. Track had not smoked cigarettes in years, but his mouth tasted too foul from medication to be able to appreciate one of his cigars. Chesterton stepped behind the wheelchair. The nurse released the brake, and Track closed his eyes, inhaling the smoke again, not wanting to think about George, but not able to think of anything else....

TRACK WAS WORKING THROUGH a package of Camel filters, the filters broken off, as Chesterton was saying to him, "I'm sorry your watch was taken from you, believe me. Should I go back and have the nurse get it from the hospital safe?"

"No, just tell me the time."

"Five minutes later than the last time. Look here, he's a very sturdy fellow, George is. And you shouldn't hold yourself responsible. You told me how it happened."

"I was covering him," Track whispered.

"The man who shot him slipped through and then you started down. It could just as easily have happened in the reverse."

"But it didn't, dammit," Track snapped. "Jesus," Track said as he stared at his right hand. It was shaking. "His mother and that low-life who—shit! Both of them dead in that accident and now George like this. Jesus, Abner, I don't—"

"Whatever happens, the only medicine for you once you're well enough for a transatlantic flight is your Desiree Goth. Forgive my bluntness, but—"

"Sir Abner—if he dies. . ." Track began slowly.

"If he dies," Chesterton interrupted, "he'll have died for what he believes in, the same as perhaps someday you'll do in this business you and George and I are in."

Track stared at the green walls of the corridor, at the gray doors with their metallic dent-plates that separated him from the operating room.

"You always let it be assumed you were doing this for the money," Chesterton continued. "But I knew you weren't. I knew why you wouldn't take the job all those times I offered it to you. You were sick of the killing, sick of the violence—man's inhumanity to man and all that, what the liberals give lip service to and men such as yourself have to live with. George—I felt it in him, too. He's like you, and if he dies because he was trying to make the world a little bit better place for people to live in, then he dies. And if you wallow in your own grief and blow this thing of blaming yourself out of all proportion, wind up shriveling up inside and dying because of it and can't do your work any longer, well—" Chesterton hesitated and Track looked at him "—well, then George will have endured this, perhaps died, all for nothing, won't he?" This oration finished, Sir Abner Chesterton pulled himself to his feet and lit a cigarette for himself, then walked away down the corridor.

Dan Track watched him go, then after a moment stubbed out the cigarette he'd been smoking and crumpled the rest of the pack in his right fist.

CHESTERTON'S COAT was off, hooked on his left thumb over his left shoulder, his wide silk tie at half mast, the sleeves of his white shirt rolled up past the elbows. He was pacing back and forth outside the operating room. After a long time Track said, "You were right."

"I know," the Englishman nodded, looking at him for a moment.

"Go to hell—but you're a good friend," Track continued.

"I know that, too—and thank you, I've already been there on more than one occasion, just as you have."

"How long has it been?"

"George has been in there for six hours. I daresay it shouldn't be that terribly much longer."

"What do you think?" Track asked, looking for reassurance.

"You mean guess?"

"Yeah, guess."

"As I declared from the outset, he's stronger than two men and he's healthy as the proverbial horse. If anyone can survive it he can. The intestinal damage is repairable. The real concern is that one fragment lodged near the heart. I'm afraid I'm a poor anatomist—they told me the part of the heart and—"

The doors leading to the operating room burst open.

"Who the hell are you?" demanded a steely-eyed gray-haired man, his face pale against a five-o'clock shadow. In his left hand he held a surgical mask and cap. The front of his green tunic was stained wet with sweat.

"I'm his uncle," Track said, nodding toward the operating theater. "How—"

"Oh, the bleeder. How's the arm?"

"Fine, fine. How—"

"God, that kid's built like a brick shithouse. His heart stopped twice, but we got it going again."

"I say, doctor, really—is the boy. . ." Chesterton began.

"He's very weak—going to be in Intensive Care for a few days—" Track felt himself suddenly bathed in sweat as the surgeon continued. "He's going to have a colostomy bag for a little while until we do the final operation. But he's a strong kid. If all my patients were like that, hell—he'll be fine unless the earth opens up and swallows the hospital."

Dan Track started to laugh—he didn't really know why.

3

It was dark outside and Track sat alone in a curtained-off area of the Intensive Care Unit with George, his eyes riveted on the machinery that monitored George's heart and respiration. He didn't know whether it was fatigue or the pain killers he was taking or the mesmerizing but reassuring blips of the monitor, but he again found his thoughts drawn back to his parents. It was years after their deaths when he learned that his father had served in the OSS during World War II. The war was the reason for the disparity between the age of Track and his dead sister Diane; she had been born before the war, he after it. In the postwar period, his father left government service and returned to his professorship. Track vaguely recalled the graduate students who would keep his father and mother and sometimes his older sister up late into the night with their talk and their ideas.

Mainly he remembered the chalkboard that he was never allowed to write on. His father's computations were always there, and sometimes they would be crossed through as if in rage. On the day he and his sister had moved from the house to live with their aunt, he had quietly gone upstairs to his father's study and erased the blackboard—forever.

Their "aunt" was really only a family friend, and turned out to be an alcoholic who had spent through their insurance money.

Track closed his eyes, remembering the way his parents had died.

It was the third day of August, 1956. Track and his mother, father and sister and himself were on a cruise ship off the coast of Florida, enjoying the vacation his mother had always wanted to have. Without warning, the ship's boilers exploded, ripping away a portion of the bottom and side of the hull. David Hunter Track had kissed him, kissed his sister and lowered them into the lifeboat filled with children. Track brought into focus a picture of David Track holding his wife in his arms, and remembered that his mother had kissed them before his father had put them in the boat. She had told them to be brave children and that mommy and daddy would be coming in another boat.

Track remembered that his father's last words were not "I love you." He had said that in everything he had ever done. He had said, "Regardless of your age, you're the man now, maybe always, if your mother and I don't make it. Take care of your sister, Dan. Now hug me."

He had hugged his father, and as the lifeboat drifted away he had watched them holding each other on the deck.

He had watched as another of the listing ship's boilers had exploded and flames engulfed the upper deck, watched as his father had drawn his mother close against him to protect his wife with his own body.

He had watched as the hull came apart in a sickening shriek, a death rattle, and the ship rolled over and sank. He remembered Diane holding him and trying to shield his eyes and he could still taste the saltiness of her tears—but he held tight to her, hearing the children scream and wail and cry around them. The crying had gone on through the night and into the next morning, and sometimes Dan Track would awaken at night when he was alone and still hear it.

The Coast Guard had come, and they had been saved. But they were orphans, and suddenly life was very different....

He realized his eyes were still closed in the darkness when he heard the gentle voice of a nurse beside him. "Major Track? Mr. Beegh's vital signs are very strong. You should go to your own bed and sleep now. Maybe you can talk with him tomorrow."

Dan Track exhaled hard. His mouth burned from the cigarettes. "All right," Track told the nurse. She was pretty, he thought, the lights from the machinery that watched over George's vital signs reflected in her dark eyes. Her dark skin was soft as she touched his hand a moment before beginning to turn his wheelchair. "All right," he said with resignation.

HIS LEFT ARM still hurt when he moved it, but no bone had been broken, and he kept kneading the white rubber ball the therapist had given him. Track sat in the chair opposite George's bed—in a private room now, no longer Intensive Care.

Track had been released two days earlier. George had awakened a few times since the night Track had sat beside him in the Intensive Care Unit, but only to mutter meaningless phrases, then drift off again.

Track's rear end hurt, and he shifted uncomfortably in the seat, glancing again at his watch—he'd been in the room for two hours.

Then he heard the voice—barely a whisper, dry sounding.

"Uncle Dan?"

"Yeah, yeah, son. I'm right here." And Track stood up and walked the three paces to stand beside the bed.

"What the hell. . ." George began.

"You were in a bad way, George, but you'll be all right now."

"I feel—what the hell—" he exclaimed, fumbling beneath the sheet with his hand.

"A colostomy bag," Track said.

"Aww, shit!"

"It's just temporary. The faster you get your strength back, then the sooner they can do the operation necessary so you won't need it. The doctor says maybe another week and they can think about trying it."

"I'm. . . a—"

"You're gonna be fine—back to normal—" and Track laughed "—or at least whatever the hell was normal for you."

"What—ahh, shit! I can't even think—"

"You rest, George. I'll—"

"What happened to your, ahh—"

"Arm?"

"Yeah, arm. Shit, I feel like I've been out on a drunk!"

"It's the medication—it'll wear off. And my arm's fine—took a slug and got a real bleeder out of it. But it's already healing—doctor says I'll be out of the sling in a few days. I got the good doctor—Chesterton fixed that. We gave you the guy who got the low grades in medical school."

"Fuck you," George said, starting to laugh. But then his face froze. "Can't do that too good—"

"It's 'too well,' and if you say it only hurts when you laugh I'll clip you." Track laughed, watching George suppress a smile.

"Hey, it's gonna be a while before we get back in the field—we get those suckers?"

Track nodded, then added, "Yeah, every one of them. You got most of them. I cleaned up after you took those slugs."

"When I was down, did I talk funny? You know—you hear about guys when they get shot or something, talking out of their heads like that—"

"You mean the bit about carrying Arnold Schwarzenegger's picture next to your heart?"

"Be serious, did I, ahh—"

"No. You were as silent as a stone, kid, silent as a stone."

George seemed to consider that for a moment, then said, "Go see Desiree, and give her a kiss for me."

"I'll give her a kiss for myself, turkey—but yeah, Chesterton's telling me the same thing. So I'm gonna go, first of next week—after we know about you and the colostomy bag."

"You don't have to wait." George grinned. "Hey, look, like a rock, huh?"

"Yeah, well, long as I've got the sling I can't hold Desiree right anyway. Besides—I'd like to make sure they don't give you the good doctor this time. That one with the funny hands was just perfect for you. He told me he was gonna be a brain surgeon. I told him lucky for him he wasn't or he wouldn't have been able to work on you, you know. But he told me—"

"What?"

Track watched his nephew's eyes. "Well,"

Track said, "he said the reason he quit being a brain surgeon was because the cost was too prohibitive. Getting those custom-made surgical gloves with ten thumbs was—"

"Go away!"

Track reached out his right hand and clasped George's shoulder. "Hey, don't go jumping any nurses in the hallways or anything, okay? That colostomy bag would get in the way anyway. You rest and I'll see ya tomorrow. You need anything, the Consortium insures the place lock, stock and barrel. You want it, you got it."

"I want Dolly Parton to give me a big hug."

"Well, almost anything you want."

"Cigarettes?"

Track had started for the door. He turned around and looked at George Beegh and laughed. "Quit cigarettes, like I told you." And Track walked from the room into the corridor and shut the door, leaning back hard against it, closing his eyes.

4

"I will be late for my conference, and you will be the one held accountable," she told the reservations clerk.

"But Comrade Ivanova, that the aircraft has experienced minor difficulties is unavoidable."

"Soviet airliners always experience minor difficulties," she snapped, and then she smiled. "Of course, it is not your fault—but how long?"

"At least another hour, Comrade—at least that."

"Is there a lounge where—"

"Wait." And he took back the ticket voucher and the travel papers on the counter top. "It is comrade Dr. Ivanova, is that not correct? A scientist at—"

"Academgorodok, yes. That is why I must fly to Berlin—there is the Congress of the Union for the Advancement of Physics. I am to address the conference this evening at the opening dinner and—"

"There is a lounge, Comrade, a very comfortable lounge for party officials and scientists. I can call someone to show you the way."

"I can find it myself. Which way—" She realized she was tapping her right boot loudly enough that she could hear it, and she flicked her eyes toward the floor, mentally ordering her foot to stop. She looked back into the face of the reservations clerk.

"The first corridor beyond the booth for the Chemical Worker's Society for Political Awareness, Comrade. You would turn left and it is the first double doors. There are complimentary beverages available."

"This is for scientists and high-ranking party officials?"

"Yes, Comrade. Why?"

She was tapping her foot again, and she shifted her weight to her right foot so she couldn't do it. "Very well." But she did not think it was very well at all. Such a lounge should be for all comrades, she thought secretly. But she said nothing—she had observed the flicker in his eyes when she had made the remark about the plane being late. "Very well," she repeated, taking her ticket and travel documents and putting them inside her purse. "My luggage?"

"It is secure, Comrade Ivanova. You will be paged by name in the lounge when your flight is ready for boarding."

"Good." She nodded, brushing back a lock of her long blond hair as it tumbled across her forehead. In her right hand she grasped the handle of her attaché case. "This I will take with me." And she started away, then turned. "Thank you for your courtesy, Comrade." She did not wait for a reply.

She started walking along the main corridor of the terminal. The Chemical Worker's Society for Political Awareness was dead ahead of her. She listened to the rhythm of her heels striking the hard floor as she walked, trying to control her temper. She was nervous enough giving the talk at the opening dinner—the delay made her stomach churn. She had been thrust into the scientific limelight owing to what she considered her minor role in working to defuse a thermonuclear device a mad Nazi named Johannes Krieger had planted at Academgorodok.

Tatiana Ivanova smiled as the woman standing beside the Chemical Worker's Society for Political Awareness booth handed her a leaflet. She made a mental note to leave it in the lounge.

She passed through an outer set of double doors leading to the lounge. Inside, there was another set of double doors and in front of them a small vestibule where an immaculately dressed army corporal sat at a desk. He snapped to attention.

Tatiana smiled at him, thinking he was handsome despite his ridiculously short haircut.

Without being asked, she handed over her travel documents and rested her attaché case on the desk top.

The corporal took a half step back and clicked

his heels as he gave her the familiar salute a soldier gives an important civilian. She had seen her father do it often enough.

"Comrade Ivanova, this way, please." The soldier smiled at her as he passed her papers back. She lowered her eyes, then raised them and smiled back, depositing her papers in the top of her bag, and started to pick up her attaché case. But the young soldier reached across and took it. "Permit me, Comrade," he said, and she nodded to him, passing through the now open doorway, the young corporal behind her.

The floor of the lounge was thickly carpeted in a shade of blue that reminded her of the skirt to her childhood school uniform. She hated the color.

Couches lined the far side of the room, and chairs were grouped around a glass-topped round table in the center. On the near side—she could smell it as she passed it—was a small bar. "I will sit there." She gestured toward the couch farthest from the bar.

The young soldier nodded, and she looked away from him. As she crossed the room, she noticed a backgammon game on the round table. Beside it was a copy of *Soviet Life*.

Tatiana stopped beside the couch, letting her fur coat fall open.

"Would there be anything else, Comrade Ivanova?" the corporal inquired.

She looked into his face. "No—but thank you.

You have been very kind. I just wish to rest before my journey."

"A pleasant journey, Comrade. You shall not be disturbed." Again he saluted as he set her case on the far end of the couch, then turned and marched smartly away.

She found herself still smiling, but shook it off as she shrugged out of her coat and threw the fur on the far edge of the couch, half obscuring her brown leather attaché case. She smoothed her skirt under her as she sank into the sofa, which was absurdly overstuffed, she thought. She looked toward the bar. "Why not," she said, laughing. Her father would certainly not pass it up.

She got up, tugging at her sweater as she crossed the room toward the bar, her eyes already scanning it for something other than vodka. There was a Scotch that she recognized as being very expensive and imported from western Europe, and she moved toward the bottle.

As she was mixing her Scotch with ice water she had found in a pitcher, she turned at the sound of the lounge doors opening. A well-dressed and very attractive, though older, woman stopped briefly on the threshold and then walked gracefully into the room. Her shoulder-length hair was a dark auburn color, and her eyes were a strange mixture of gray and brown beneath the artificial lights of the lounge.

"Hello," the woman said, looking at Tatiana.

Her accented Russian was good, but clearly not native.

"Hello," Tatiana replied. "Would you like a drink? It seems I'm behind the bar."

The woman laughed, nodding. "Yes, if there's something besides vodka."

"Scotch," Tatiana said, holding the bottle aloft. The woman's clothes were expensive and very Western—the tight skirt, the expensive-looking high heels, the short waist-length fur jacket. Tatiana guessed the woman's age at perhaps early forties, but she seemed at once younger and older. The woman's smile was gone as she started across the room. "Would you like water if you want Scotch?" Tatiana asked.

"Oh, I'm sorry," the woman said, setting her attaché case, her purse and her coat on the couch beside the one Tatiana had used. "Yes, please—but not too much water."

Tatiana watched the woman start back across the room. She hoped that when she was this woman's age she would carry herself as well.

The woman sat opposite her at the bar. "Your flight delayed, too?"

"Yes—to Berlin. And yours?"

"Oh, farther away than that," the woman said as she smiled noncommittally and looked into her purse. "Cigarette?"

"No—thank you." Tatiana smiled, setting a drink in front of the woman. "My name is Tatiana—Tatiana Ivanova."

"I'm Janet Tilman—hello." And Janet Tilman extended her right hand. Tatiana took it.

"You are not Russian?" Tatiana asked.

"Canadian—by birth. But my soul is Russian, honestly." She laughed a little laugh that Tatiana thought sounded odd. "My husband and I have been here for a long time. We moved here to work for peace."

"Oh, well." Tatiana didn't know what to say. She ducked once more to put away the ice water, and the heel of her boot caught in the hem of her skirt as she stood, making a ripping sound. "Oh, blast! My skirt—"

"I've got a small sewing kit in my attaché case," Janet Tilman volunteered. "I can fix it for you. I used to be very good at sewing—honestly."

Tatiana started to protest, and then simply said, "Thank you," and smiled.

"Come on—bring your drink and we can talk." And Janet Tilman was up from the bar stool and stubbing out her cigarette in the ashtray.

"All right," Tatiana smiled. "But please, speak English. I could use the practice."

"I will then." Janet Tilman sat on the edge of the couch and opened her attaché case.

"Where do you want me to stand?" Tatiana asked her.

"Let's see.... Why don't you just look toward the doors for a minute."

Tatiana did as she was told, finding herself liking the woman. But the eyes—there was something about them. Janet Tilman was chattering now at full speed, and Tatiana found herself smiling.

"Years ago," Janet Tilman was saying, "we were poor and I used to sew a lot. I made a lot of my son's clothes—cut them down from hand-me-downs."

"What are hand-me-downs?"

"Things someone else has no use for that maybe you can use. This is a pretty skirt."

"Your son—what does he do?"

Tatiana felt the woman's hands leave the skirt, and she turned to look at her. "Look out for the needle," the woman murmured soullessly.

"Did I. . ." Tatiana began.

"My son is dead," she whispered.

Tatiana turned fully now to look at her. "I'm so sorry—I truly am. Was it recent?"

"No, it was ten years ago."

"An accident?"

"No! No. . .he was murdered. By my brother. Because of my husband's beliefs, my brother killed our son and tried to kill us."

"My heart—it leaves out for you—"

"Goes—goes out—"

"Your brother was punished for this horrible thing?"

Janet Tilman's eyes lowered. "No," she barely whispered. "He was never punished. We lived in Canada, but my brother was a high-ranking member of the United States Army. They covered up the murder so he could go free. He was some sort of secret policeman."

"You poor woman. This is—" Tatiana couldn't find the right word and she began searching for it.

"Here," the woman said, setting down the sewing kit and turning to her open attaché case. "After he killed my son and tried to murder my husband and me, my brother burned down our house. We lost everything that we had—except this." She opened the expandable file built into the attaché-case lid. She extracted a very thin book-size leather portfolio. Inside it was a photo beneath a piece of clear vinyl. "I have the original at our home, where my husband and I work. I help him with his work—we work for peace. To make a world where such a thing cannot happen."

Tatiana stared at the photograph, hearing Janet Tilman as she spoke. "This is my son. He was fifteen then. And this is my husband, Morton. Dr. Morton Tilman. Our son's name was David, named after my father. And this other man, he's my brother. The man who killed my son."

Tatiana looked at the photograph and then at the eyes of the woman. They were washed with tears and somehow the tears made their color more clear. Tatiana Ivanova knew the eyes—they were the same eyes that stared out of the photograph. She had seen these eyes before, very closely, seen the resolve in them, resolve mixed with anger and frustration and determined purpose. She knew the eyes and she knew the man. He was the American major, Dan Track.

"This man, your...your brother," Tatiana whispered. "He did this thing? He killed your son?"

"Yes," Janet Tilman answered.

Tatiana felt a strange tightness in her chest, and suddenly she was very afraid.

5

"And it has fallen to the scientist, the physicist in particular, to dare to imagine the impossible and then to make it possible. Thank you." Tatiana looked up from her note cards, removed her glasses and smiled as the assembled physicists from all the Soviet-aligned nations and many of the Third World nations, as well, began to applaud her.

She sensed the movement to her left and turned as the chairman of the Congress of the Union for the Advancement of Physics stretched his arms toward her, embraced her and planted a wet kiss on each of her cheeks, then shook her hand in both of his meaty paws.

She turned to acknowledge the applause of her fellow physicists and smiled again. She wondered if they had really liked her speech or if they perhaps felt obligated to applaud because of her recent notoriety within the scientific community. Perhaps they only applauded because she was a blond-haired woman in her early twenties and they were used to stoop-shouldered old men with balding pates and brushy mustaches.

"Thank you, Comrade Ivanova. Your talk—it cannot be described, Comrade," said her host, bringing her out of her thoughts.

"Thank you," she said, smiling at the chairman of the congress. Then she turned away from the speaker's rostrum and found her seat at the long head table. A waiter came forward and bent down to her. "Yes?" she asked.

"Comrade Dr. Ivanova, the gentleman at the very rear of the hall has asked you be told he requests the honor of purchasing you a drink."

"He what? I don't know—"

"The gentleman gave me this card," the waiter said, indicating a white rectangle on the silver tray he carried. Tatiana picked up the card and read, "Sergei Baslovitch, Major" and then beneath it in smaller capitals, "Committee for State Security."

Tatiana looked into the eyes of the waiter. "Tell the comrade yes, as soon as the meeting is formally closed."

"Major Baslovitch instructed me, Comrade, to say he would meet you in the hotel bar."

She had never met a man in a bar before, but she nodded and opened the small beaded bag beside her plate and placed the business card inside, then placed the bag on her lap.

SERGEI BASLOVITCH felt slightly stupid wearing dark glasses in a dimly lit bar. Everyone would think he was trying to look like some sort of spy. Which was amusing to him since he was indeed some sort of spy. He shrugged away the thought and returned to his vodka. His eyes, seared in the explosion outside Academgorodok, were healing, but light, however dim, still irritated them. The bar lights, though low, were harsh and he had put on the dark glasses when he had suddenly found his eyes bothering him.

Baslovitch glanced at his watch. It read eleven thirty-six. He had reset it to East German time when first arriving at the conference because he would be out of Russia for several days on this and other business. Baslovitch shifted his weight on the bar stool, glancing down at his coat to make certain that the Heckler & Koch 9mm wasn't showing in the shoulder holster.

He lit a cigarette—a Lucky. American cigarettes were one of his passions that his position with the KGB allowed him to exercise at will. He was on the point of deciding that the girl was not coming—after all, he was probably an old man to her, almost twenty years her senior—when he heard her voice, "Comrade Major Baslovitch? It's good to see you."

He turned on his stool and stood. Thin straps were all that appeared to prevent her white dress from defying gravity, and despite the crocheted shawl around her shoulders, he could see more of her than he had seen at Academgorodok.

"You are lovely," he said, smiling. "A very lovely girl."

"Why would you invite a girl to meet you in a bar, Comrade? Would not a woman be better?"

He felt himself smiling at her, and he removed his dark glasses in spite of the light. Now he could see her striking green eyes, and he knew he was falling under her spell. He was playing a fool's game. "I think we can find a table. May I buy you that drink?"

"All right, I'd like that." She nodded, laughing a little.

"Why do you laugh?" he asked her, guiding her by her right elbow toward a table in the far corner of the room. As his fingertips touched her skin, he could feel his heart racing. "Why do you laugh?" Baslovitch repeated, smiling.

"That such a sophisticated man as yourself should offer to buy me a drink, I suppose," she said, as she looked up at him and cocked her head.

Baslovitch caught the eye of a waiter as they wove their way toward the table, asking Tatiana Ivanova, "What would you like to drink?"

"I like Scotch—real Scotch—but I know that's terribly expensive."

"Chivas Regal for the lady, and another vodka for me." He turned away from the waiter.

They had reached the table, and he asked her, "May I help you with your shawl?"

"It's a little cool—I think I'll wear it," she replied, and he stood until she sat and then slid into the leather-covered bench opposite her. "Why did you ask me to join you?" she said over the table.

He laughed, his eyes still bothering him. "A familiar face that had seemed friendly once and seems friendly now. For a man in my profession that is a luxury, Comrade."

"Why? I can't understand that...I mean—never mind."

"No, say what you wish to say."

She looked down at her small delicate hands, and then her eyes drifted up toward his. "I know that sometimes the KGB is rumored to do some things that—" She didn't finish.

Sergei Baslovitch felt in a reckless mood. "Sometimes these things are not rumors. But I am not a secret policeman. I work in counterespionage—I have always." The drinks arrived and he changed the subject. "The weather here is very cool for this time of year. I hope you brought a warm coat, Comrade."

"Yes, I did bring a warm coat—and did you?" And she laughed.

When the waiter was gone, she laughed even louder and Baslovitch suddenly reached out his right hand and touched her fingertips. She did not withdraw her hand. "I am," he whispered, "not someone who knocks on doors in the middle of the night and hauls away political dissidents to oblivion. I never have been."

"I couldn't picture you doing such things. Your eyes—how are—"

"How are they?" And he took the dark glasses from his outside breast pocket.

"Is it the light? I notice they're red."

"Yes, it's the light. But the doctors—" he lit another cigarette "—tell me it is getting better and I know that it is. Soon I will not even need these at all." He set the glasses on the table. "Would you like a cigarette?"

"I do not smoke."

"Smart of you." He watched as she picked up his glasses and looked at them a moment.

"Put them on—to help your eyes," she said, and he shrugged, taking them from her, imagining they felt warm with her touch. He put them on. "You look very handsome in them."

"I look stupid in them. The only time I can safely be without them is when I sleep." And suddenly he felt very awkward having said that. "I did not—"

"I would like to see you without your glasses again, then," Tatiana said. Baslovitch looked at her. Her eyes held a frankness and a prettiness he had not seen for a very long time.

"You are only a girl. . . " he began.

"Then why did you invite me—if I am only a girl?"

Baslovitch said nothing, and she continued. "I think that you are a good man—and I thought of you that night alone in my bed, because you might have been permanently blinded, because you were so brave to go back after the American."

"Dan Track," he murmured.

"I prayed for you—so there." She laughed. "I am not a good Communist after all."

Baslovitch laughed. "Then I am not a good Communist either, because I, too, prayed that my vision would be restored."

Her left hand closed over his right. "You are a hero, but more than that, I think—"

"I did what I had to do."

"Rescuing the American was not part of that."

"He saved thousands of lives—he didn't have to do that. He could have walked away."

"Then the two of you are very much alike, because you had no reason to go in after him and risk your own life."

He didn't know what to say.

Tatiana spoke again, her voice sounding uncertain. "If you would like me to sleep with you, I would like that, too—very much, I think."

He half finished his vodka, leaving the rest. "Tatiana, you are the loveliest woman I have ever known—"

"Don't lie to me." She smiled. "I'm a very average-looking girl. I'm wearing a very pretty dress and I arranged my hair very carefully tonight, but that is all."

He took the glasses from his face and offered them to her. "Then it is you who needs the help with your vision."

HE HAD SLIPPED between her thighs twice that night, and the gray light that filtered through the curtains of his hotel room had awakened him and he watched her now as she slept. Such a thin body, the breasts tiny, warm when he had touched them, rested his head against them. He gazed down at the look of innocence on her face. He whispered the words because she was asleep and he knew she would not hear him. "I could have loved you a long time ago." He looked away from her and closed his eyes against the dawn light....

FOR HER SAFETY, they had left the hotel by separate exits ten minutes apart, and he waited for her now in the small restaurant where they were to meet for breakfast. She was late, and he chided himself for staring at his watch like a teenager in love. Perhaps, he thought, she had not been pleased with him. Perhaps he really was too old for her. Of course he was, he told himself. A passion for a young girl was the first sign of middle age in a man.

And suddenly Tatiana was there beside him, saying hello and sliding into the booth. The waitress arrived instantly, and Tatiana ordered coffee and orange juice. He ordered the same. "You look beautiful," he said. As she shrugged out of her fur coat, her hair fell past the shoulders of her gray sweater. The sweater had a cowl neck, and he could see the slenderness of her throat.

"I must hurry a little or I will be late for the congress," she said. "The formal meeting is this morning and—"

"May I see you again?" Baslovitch cut in.

"You said you were leaving later today."

"My business is over—I was following someone at your conference."

"Not me?"

He laughed as the waitress set down the coffee and the orange juice. He sipped the juice. It was terribly watered down. "No, not you. I would follow you by choice, not under orders."

Tatiana smiled. "You could come to Academgorodok—"

"I am sure you have a lover there—you know, a special friend."

"I do not. Will you come?"

"Yes," Baslovitch answered. "And if I do not come it is because I cannot come, not because I would not. But I will come."

"There...there is something I must tell you," Tatiana began.

Baslovitch felt a tightness in his throat. There were always things he needed to be told. "There is nothing you *must* tell me."

"No, I must tell you. Last night I came to have the drink with you because I saw it as an opportunity to tell someone I felt I could trust something very important. I met a woman at the airport in Moscow. What she told me, and the picture she showed to me, frightened me. On the airplane, I thought of you as being someone I could trust to tell this to if somehow I could find you. And then you sent the waiter with your card and—"

He exhaled loudly. "I see, then—"

"But no—you see, after I saw you, well, I wanted very much for you to be my lover. And I realized that was why I was thinking of you."

He looked at her as she knitted her fingertips together.

"The woman's name was Janet Tilman, and she told me she was Canadian and that she left Canada many years ago to come to our country to work for peace. Her husband's name I do not remember. But she showed me a picture of three men—her husband, her son and her brother—and told me that her son was dead, murdered by her brother, who was in the secret police of the American Army." She cleared her throat and sipped her juice before going on. "She said that her brother was not punished for his crime. But the name of the brother was all wrong!"

"What do you mean, all wrong?"

"She told me that he murdered their son, attempted to murder her and her husband and burned their home to the ground. Apparently he did this because of their political beliefs. I got the impression from talking with her that her husband is a scientist, and that she helps him in his work."

"What do you mean, all wrong?" Baslovitch repeated.

"The woman's eyes—they were the same, I remembered them."

"The same as whose?" Baslovitch said just a bit impatiently.

"The eyes of the woman were the same as the eyes of the man in the photograph she called her brother—so she must be his sister."

"You aren't making any sense," Baslovitch said.

Tatiana was staring down at her hands, then raised her eyes to his. "The man in the photograph, Sergei, was Dan Track, and she said that he murdered her son!"

TATIANA MISSED the morning session of the meeting. Baslovitch contacted security for the congress and informed them he was interviewing her for information necessary to one of his investigations, but that she was in no way implicated. Indeed, he had said, she was as loyal a Communist as could be found. They had walked afterward, then taken Baslovitch's car out into the chilled autumn countryside, parked the car and walked some more. She stood shivering, even in her fur. Baslovitch got up from the deadfall log on which he sat, removed his khaki trench coat and over her protestations draped it across her shoulders. "I am sorry," he said, "but we are safe out here, at least. You are certain?"

"The man in the photo was Dan Track," she whispered. "Hold me, Sergei." Baslovitch folded her into his arms and held her head against his chest.

"I will always hold you," he told her quietly, touching his lips to her forehead.

"What should we do?"

He let go of her shoulders and held her at arm's length. With the tips of his fingers of his right hand, he raised her chin so he could see her eyes. "Why do you cry?"

"I should not have told you this thing. Inside of me I feel that something—"

"That something bad will come of it?"

"Yes."

"You are probably right. But I must look into this, and I must follow it where it leads me. After all—" he laughed, letting go of her chin "—you called me a hero. Would you expect less from a hero?"

"I had to—"

"You have told somebody. Tell no one else. If it is possible, I will tell you what I learn. Perhaps you were wrong—for all our sakes I hope that."

"I can't believe that Dan Track could do what this woman said."

"Men do things they are often not proud of in the doing, or afterward," he told her, shaking his head. He lit a cigarette.

"Do those things make you warm?" she asked.

"No," he answered flatly. "I agree with you. I do not think Major Track would have done such a thing—kill his nephew, attempt to murder his sister and brother-in-law—which means there is something very wrong, Tatiana. If this Janet Tilman is indeed Track's sister, what on earth is she doing in the Soviet Union?"

"If there is something he should know—"

"Will I tell Dan Track?" He shook his head, staring at his shoes for a moment, then looked into her eyes. "I will tell him, very probably. Which is very stupid of me. But I learned that honor is not a word for capitalists only. You must say nothing of this. Ever again. Promise me?"

"I promise you," she whispered, leaning against him. He raised her chin and lowered his mouth against hers, tasting her lips. "And I promise you this, too," she whispered as he looked at her. She raised herself on her toes and folded her arms about his neck and kissed him.

6

Announcements crackled over the airport PA system in French, German and English as Track left passport control, carrying his stuff sack and his attaché case. His eyes began scanning the terminal building; the figure he searched for would not be that difficult to find. The giant black man Desiree Goth called Zulu, his real name something Track couldn't even guess, stood at least six-foot-six, maybe taller. Even in a suit, Zulu's body appeared rippled with muscles. His head was completely bald.

Track reflected on the current state of his relationship with Zulu. They were friendly enemies, the emphasis on the enemies part, he thought. He sensed that Zulu saw him as a danger to Desiree Goth, and the thought crossed Track's mind that Zulu loved her, too.

Dan Track kept walking, warm in his bomber jacket and the heavy sweater, but knowing that in the mountains beyond it would be cold.

He kept searching the crowd, not seeing Zulu but suddenly hearing a feminine voice call his name. "Dan!"

Track turned, and in that moment, Desiree Goth hurtled into his arms and all he could see was the raven blackness of her hair. Her arms folded about his neck. "Dan! Oh, I love you so much," she whispered, and Dan Track dropped his case and crushed her against him, the fingers of his right hand knotting into her hair, cocking her head back, his mouth coming down on hers.

Then he let go of her so he could look at her. Her black-gloved hands touched his face, and he could smell the leather mingled with the scent of her perfume. Track moved his left arm too fast and winced. "It still bothers you?" Desiree asked, her voice soft and concerned.

"A little."

"And George?"

"The operation was a success. He should be up and around in ten days or so, but he'll have to take it easy. And he got rid of the bag—that's what he's happy about," Track told her, holding her hands in his.

"Major!" a strong voice boomed.

Track looked across Desiree's shoulders, then drew her close against him with his left arm. Another spasm of pain shook him, but it wasn't something he couldn't live with.

The voice, very British sounding but deep like that of an operatic baritone, thundered again. "I shan't say it is a pleasure to see you again—I consider us both men who value truth." Zulu extended his right hand. Track took it, expecting the worst, but it was not a crusher handshake, only firm, dry.

"Well, I won't say it's good to see you, either," Track responded. "You doing okay, Zulu?"

"Admirably, Major." He emphasized the military title. Track had given up asking the huge African to abandon it. "And your arm?"

"Admirable," Track said, smiling.

"And your nephew—the lad named George?"

"Admirable, as well."

"Excellent. I've arranged for your luggage to be transferred to the Mercedes."

"The two of you—" Desiree laughed "—should be friends after all we've been through."

Zulu looked at her, Track noting the expression as one of genuine puzzlement. "Odd you should say that, Miss Desiree," Zulu said as she linked her left arm through his right, then her right arm through Track's left. Desiree started forward, and the crowd of passengers parted as the Red Sea had parted for Moses as Zulu edged slightly ahead.

"The two men I care most about should be friends," she insisted, smiling.

"I am touched, Miss Desiree—and should be is definitely the correct phrasing."

Track looked at Zulu and laughed....

THE DRIVE past the Swiss cuckoo-clock houses had been uneventful. Desiree asked Track for the details of the fight in which both he and George had been injured, and Track filled her in on the background of the aircraft theft ring. Desiree talked then about her business, but only in the most general terms, Track realized. He was, after all, a lawman, in a loose sense. And Desiree Angelique Goth was a criminal in more than a loose sense. She was responsible for various arms and munitions thefts that Track personally knew of, and many others that he didn't want to know about. She'd sold arms on the black market, internationally, for more years than he would have thought possible, considering her relative youth, dealing to anyone with the money to pay.

Zulu, at Desiree's insistence, had joined them for a late lunch and was being his usual taciturn self, Track thought.

But he had broken his silence when Desiree had mentioned that she was becoming more selective in her clientele.

Track had looked at him across his wineglass. "I gather you disapprove?"

"The morality of Miss Desiree's business affairs rarely concerns me, Major. But the practicality of them does, I'm afraid."

"That's enough, Zulu."

"As you will, miss." Zulu fell silent again.

It was later now, and the winter sun was dipping behind the mountains in the distance. Track zipped the front of his battered brown leather bomber jacket with his left hand, his right arm snugged around Desiree's waist. Her hands were smothered in a fur muff, the muff a perfect match for the mink coat she wore. She had changed from the black dress she had worn earlier to loose-fitting gray slacks, stuffed into the tops of high black-leather boots. The effect, considering the red, long-sleeved blouse she wore, was very Cossack-like. Track realized he was watching her, thinking about her rather than listening to her.

"I'm sorry—I didn't hear what you were saying."

"Your mind is somewhere else," she whispered. A low wind moaned down from the mountains, whistling once in a while through the pine boughs.

"I was just thinking about you—"

"I'm vain enough to accept that, but what, or should I say who, else is in your thoughts?"

Track laughed.

"Go ahead and light one of your awful cigars," she told him. "The smell won't bother me. Actually they're quite pleasant smelling, as cigars go, and we're outside, anyway."

"All right." Track took a Cuesta-Rey Six-T from his cigar case, guillotined the tip and dug into his pocket for his lighter. He cupped his gloved left hand around the flame as he drew the fire into the tobacco. Before putting away the lighter, he asked, "Do you want a cigarette?"

"Not just now. Tell me."

"All right," he said again, looking down at the

patchy snow beneath his feet. "It's this thing with George—I almost got him killed."

"He does what he does by choice, Dan."

"Yeah, well, maybe that's the trouble. He never had that much choice. Ever since he was a little boy—hell, I used to change his diapers—"

Desiree laughed, bending forward with it, her muffed hands clasped against her abdomen.

"What's so funny?" Dan Track asked her.

"Just picturing you changing diapers—especially for George."

"Let me tell you, that kid could really make the messes," Track said, and Desiree laughed again.

Track began then to tell her what he had planned to tell her, but hadn't quite known how to begin—the death of his parents, his sister caring for him, his sister marrying Robert Beegh when she was only eighteen, and the escape from the alcoholic aunt, who had spent every dime they had on booze. In the end Track said, "It was out of the frying pan and into the fire." He told her of his days in Chicago, in the gangs, of his brushes with the law and the struggle to stay alive, of doing whatever needed to be done in order to keep food on the table for his sister and her young son. Then he talked about the death of Diane and Robert Beegh and having George to look out for, keeping George with him for six months in Europe, realizing that the life of an unmarried Army captain who often went undercover for weeks at a time was no life for a teenager. He told her of the military academy he had put George through for the remaining years of high school, of George joining the Air Force, rejecting the offer of college.

And Dan Track told her other things—how he sometimes awakened at night and heard the cries of the children in the lifeboat with him and his sister. Desiree took one of her bare hands from the muff and touched his face. "I heard the nightmares," she said. "I never asked you why. I always hoped you would tell me."

"I talk in my sleep?"

"Only once. I wish I—"

He bent over her, crushing her mouth beneath his. . . .

THE GLOW of logs burning in the fireplace was all that illuminated Desiree's private apartment on the second floor of her house. Track sat with her on the floor before it, a glass of Seagram's Seven over ice in his right hand. The smoke from her cigarette had a ghostly quality as it dissipated into the darkness beyond the glow of the hearth. "We are very much alike," Desiree said. "Orphans, growing up simply because we were too stubborn to give up and die."

"I guess we are," Track said, smiling as he took the cigarette from her fingertips and inhaled the smoke deep into his lungs.

"I wish . . ." she began.

"What do you wish?"

"When we watched the stars tonight," she whispered, not looking at him. But he looked at her, her body swathed in the white linen robe, a quilt tossed over her legs against the night chill, her head leaning against the seat of the sofa. He edged slightly closer to her across the fur rug.

"What do you wish?" he repeated softly.

"That there was someplace where I would have no one to sell arms to, and you would have no terrorists or criminals you needed to pursue. Where we could just be together."

"I know," he whispered, stubbing out her cigarette in the ashtray, setting down his glass. He took her in his arms, kissing her lightly, leaning her back across the rug, feeling her hands move across him to undo the belt that held his bathrobe closed. His hands lingered beneath the quilt as they crossed the warm flesh of her legs, moving upward, slowly, searching.

Her robe opened and he slipped between her thighs. Her hands left him for a moment, then he felt the warmth of the quilt as she pulled it over them both. His lips brushed the nipple of her breast, then caressed her neck. There was a triangle of freckles beneath her left breast, and he found it and kissed it. He felt her hands on him, felt the growing hardness of his body as he slipped inside her and she whispered, "I love you, Dan." Track arched her body toward him, his hands on her, his lips touching her, his flesh against hers.

7

The flight from Berlin had been tiring. A party official he knew slightly had sat beside him, and Baslovitch had been regaled with hours of rhetoric signifying nothing. After landing, he had driven an official car from the airport parking lot, the car slow to start from days of disuse and icy cold inside, the heat working badly as it always did just when heat was needed the most. But the streets of Moscow had been deserted as he had followed the spiderweb of boulevards. He had parked in the underground garage of a building just beyond Children's World in Derzhinsky Square, and traveled up in the service elevator.

He had checked into his office, and began to dictate into a tape recorder his reports on the attempts by American and British agents to purchase in advance of the Physics Congress official transcripts of the meetings.

But other concerns pressed heavily on his mind.

He pushed the stop button on his cassette recorder, stood and walked over to his window, looking out on the children's skating arena on the square. No children were there now—it was barely dawn. The reminder of the hour made him rub the stubble on his face, and he returned to his desk and took the electric razor from the bottom drawer and plugged it in.

He began to shave, still standing, using no mirror, the razor in his right hand. With his left hand, he very slowly, very gently lifted aside the painting of V.I. Lenin that dominated the wall behind his desk. He did not care for the painting—it made Lenin look like the devil himself—but he had inherited it with the office and decided the wiser course was not to remove it.

Beneath the painting he found what he knew would be there—a small, gold-colored microphone, very flat. A wire led from it through a tiny hole in the wall.

Baslovitch smiled. There would be other devices—light-gathering optical fibers to see even now what he did and to photograph him for record. Colonel Yehrevhenskiy was spying on him again.

He eased the painting back to cover the microphone and finished shaving, putting the razor away in his drawer. Beside the razor was his second pistol that he occasionally carried when in the field in rugged terrain—a Walther P-38, marked P-1, a postwar police and military model used in West Germany. He had had the feed ramp throated to reliably handle hollowpoints. He opened the full-flap holster and removed the pistol, checking for an empty chamber, after removing the magazine. The chamber was empty. The primary magazine and the spare magazine were fully charged with eight rounds of 115-grain JHPs.

He replaced the Walther in the holster and put the holstered pistol and its black leather belt inside his attaché case, closed the case and stood up from behind the desk.

Carrying the case, he started into the hallway and down the corridor, away from his superior's office. Yehrevhenskiy would not be in yet, anyway. Since his promotion to deputy director of Covert Operations, he had taken to being a late riser. Yehrevhenskiy's superior, Commissar Ghermahnyevitch, on the other hand, was an early riser, and as Baslovitch walked past his door he walked on tiptoe. But no light emitted from the gap between the bottom of the door and the floor.

Baslovitch walked on, taking the stairwell down two floors to the computer rooms. Little high-technology equipment was housed in the old building; the computer was an information retrieval system only, and someone had once told him how many bits or bytes, or whatever they were called, the machinery was capable of. Baslovitch had then promptly and intentionally forgotten the information.

But he knew how to make a computer give up its secrets—the taking of secrets was his stock in trade. Two guards stood lazily at the door of the computer room. Baslovitch stopped in front of them, and the senior man saluted him. He nodded. "I need background information on an American who may be working with British intelligence to sabotage our conference in Berlin. I must pass."

The senior man saluted again. "This way, Comrade Major," he said, dropping the salute to unlock the door.

Baslovitch nodded again and stepped inside, donning his sunglasses as the corporal flicked the light switch. Baslovitch outwardly ignored the corporal and started toward the computer console. He sat down and activated the power for the computer.

The first name he entered through the keyboard was Track, Daniel H. He waited while the terminal display began to fill up with green, phosphorescent letters. The mysteries of computers eluded him, but he knew they were the gods of a new religion, and someday would have to be learned. As the screen continued to fill, Baslovitch read on.

> Track, Daniel H. (Hunter), born Chicago, Illinois, USA, June 21, 1948.
>
> Father: David Hunter Track, born Manchester, New Hampshire, USA, October 5, 1910; deceased, 1956.
>
> Mother: Elizabeth MacDowell Bonner (Betty), born Boston, Massachusetts, USA, November 1, 1912, married David Hunter Track, November 3, 1936, Chicago; deceased, 1956.

Sister: Diane Bonner Beegh, nee Track, born Chicago, Illinois, USA, May 18, 1940, married Robert Arlington Beegh, May 19, 1958, Chicago; deceased with husband, 1974. One son, George Woodrow Beegh.

Baslovitch punched up other relatives.

Nephew: George Woodrow Beegh, born Chicago, Illinois, USA, December 23, 1959, son of Robert and Diane, nee Track, Beegh.

The rest of the data on George Beegh followed, but nothing indicating a death date. Just as it should have been.

He read through as much of the information as he deemed necessary. Spying was no excuse for prying, he thought in English, amused with the rhyme. He voided the program and punched in Janet Tilman.

Her name was cross-referenced to Morton P. Tilman.

He punched in Morton P. Tilman.

Tilman, Morton Peter, born Toronto, Ontario, Canada, June 9, 1936.

No further data appeared, but a code reference did. Baslovitch recognized it as an eyes-only security code that Ghermahnyevitch could access, but not Colonel Yehrevhenskiy.

He punched up the code clearance. A list of names appeared, including Ghermahnyevitch's and several others, some recognizable to Baslovitch, some not, some surprising him.

One name seemed particularly odd.

Baslovitch punched up Phillip R. Laughton.

> Laughton, Phillip Rausch, born London, U.K., October 4, 1916.

Baslovitch kept reading. Apparently Laughton had defected England to Nazi Germany, 1938, serving under Wilhelm Kreutz, M.D., Ph.D. Again a code classification—the same one.

Baslovitch punched up Wilhelm Kreutz.

A full biography appeared, with several cross references. Kreutz, Baslovitch read, had supervised Nazi experiments conducted with subjects taken from the death camps, the experiments involving the use of the human mind in intelligence gathering, sabotage, remote viewing and advanced mind-control techniques.

Baslovitch shut down the machine, eyeing the monitoring camera that taped him in the facility. There would be no record he had run the programs—of that he was reasonably sure. But he already had a cover story in mind in case he was questioned.

Under his breath, he said one word—the name of a place very far away.

Baslovitch walked from the room.

8

The bed beside him was no longer warm as Track rolled over and opened his eyes. Desiree was gone.

Dan Track sat up and looked around her room. After making love on the rug in front of the fire, they had gone to her bed, after a time making love again, then falling asleep holding each other.

He pushed back the satin sheet and the down comforter, swung his legs down from the bed and stood up naked beside it.

He paced the room, searching for his robe, remembering then that he had left it beside the couch. But it wasn't there. Neither was hers.

He gave up on his robe and walked through the open connecting doors to his own smaller suite. He walked into the bathroom and stared at his face in the mirror. He needed a shave badly despite the fact that less than twenty-four hours had passed since the last one.

It had been the sunlight that had awakened him, he decided, still feeling as though he could return to their bed and sleep another ten hours.

His things had been unpacked and placed in

their respective drawers and closets, and he pulled on some underwear and a pair of Levi's that had seen better days. Barefoot and shirtless, he left his rooms and started down the hallway toward the stairs and the main floor. Gunther, the butler, smiled and said, "Guten Morgen, Herr Track."

"Guten Morgen, Gunther. Can I round up some breakfast in a little while?"

"Certainly, sir—whenever the master is ready."

"Right." Track nodded. He started down to the ground floor, heading for the gymnasium and the pool.

He skinned out of his jeans and underwear and into some swimming trunks and started for the pool. The pool was only slightly smaller than Olympic size, and above it glass panels provided insulation against the cold yet allowed diffused sunlight to warm the air. The water was electrically heated. He dived in, finally awake, treading water for a moment. He would swim for a while to get the kinks out, then the weight room for a little while for a workout on the bag, taking it easy on his injured arm. He didn't worry about Desiree—she had a business to run even when he was with her.

Then another swim, followed by breakfast.

Elvira, the cook, was very good.

AN HOUR and ten minutes after hitting the pool, he had shaved, showered, brushed, flossed, dressed and was working on the fresh coffee cake Elvira had prepared, knowing he liked it, instructed to do so by Desiree. As Gunther poured more coffee, Track asked him, "I give up, Gunther—where is Fräulein Goth?"

"Earlier she was in her office, sir. Fräulein Goth instructed the staff that your sleep should be uninterrupted. I believe the *Fräulein* is now about the grounds with Herr Zulu."

"Herr Zulu—right," Track muttered as Gunther vanished.

Feeling as though he should have done more curls in the weight room and an extra half-dozen laps in the pool, he pushed himself away from the table and stood, downing the last of his coffee and starting across the dining room into the hall, toward the front doors.

He grabbed his bomber jacket from the hall tree and pulled it on as he started through the front doors, walked across the small porch and down the three steps to the gravel driveway. The fountain ahead of him was turned off; the night temperatures were too cold. He walked along toward the front gates, not sticking to the road but rather paralleling it, walking on the snow-splotched but still green grass. As he passed beyond the bordering hedgerows, he could see Desiree just ahead, and with her the muscular, very erect giant, Zulu.

As Track drew nearer, he could see them in

greater definition. Desiree wore brown leather boots, a brown tweed full-length skirt, a heavy cowl-necked camel-colored sweater and a brown tweed stole about her shoulders.

Zulu looked the epitome of the gentleman in his tweed sport coat and gray flannel slacks. He was smoking a pipe.

"Hi!" Track said as he walked up. "I missed you guys—well, at least I missed Desiree," he said, nodding to Zulu.

Desiree waved. Zulu began to inspect his pipe. Track lit his first cigar of the day as he narrowed the gap between them and stopped. Desiree leaned forward, kissing Track's cheek and hugging the shawl closer around her.

"Why so cheerful?" Track asked, beginning to feel that he was intruding.

"Nothing to be concerned about." Desiree smiled.

Zulu cleared his throat lightly, then he began. "One of the fringe benefits of Miss Desiree's new policies, in all candor inaugurated because of her affection for you—something I cannot fathom."

"Zulu!" Desiree muttered the word through her teeth, her black hair caught in a gust of wind that molded her skirt against her legs. She turned slightly, looking neither at Track nor Zulu. Track watched her face. "Zulu exaggerates," she said.

Zulu spoke again, reaching under his jacket as he did, his left hand reappearing with what Track recognized as a Walther P-5 9mm pistol. "Suffice it to say," Zulu said, "that you might find yourself needing this as the day progresses, Major. My GP," Zulu said, referring to his Browning Hi-Power 9mm by the more European designation, GP for *grande puissance,* "should get me safely to the house. This was only a spare. And speaking of spares, you'll find extra loaded magazines on the top shelf of the credenza in the main hall. If you'll both forgive me, I've duties to which I must attend." And he extended the pistol, butt first, toward Track. Track's right hand closed around it. Zulu glanced toward Desiree and bowed ever so slightly, touching the fingertips of his right hand to the bill of his cap. "Miss Desiree—by your leave." He turned and started along the gravel driveway toward the house.

Track watched the huge Oxford-educated African for a moment, feeling the wind more bitingly cold than he had only a minute before. He felt the pressure of Desiree's hands on his left arm and he turned to look down into her blue eyes, the Walther still held easily in his right fist. "What the hell's going on?" he asked.

"I hadn't wanted Zulu to alarm you. I know you need a rest from the life you normally lead and—"

"Skip that and just tell me what the hell's going on," Track said, realizing he was sounding just a little impatient. Track slipped the Walther into his jacket pocket and brought both of his hands to Desiree's shoulders. She hesitated for an instant, then sagged against him, coming into his arms. He held her there, very quietly for a long time, feeling the spiderweb softness of her hair as tiny strands of it caught in the wind and brushed against his cheek, against his chin, against his lips. "What's wrong?" he whispered.

Her head was still against his chest, her voice barely audible. He leaned his head close against hers, touching his lips to her hair as she spoke. "One of my former clients—he's, well, he's quite upset. The road leading up to the house has been cut off. Zulu was driving down to the village and had to turn back. It appears there was an avalanche, but the conditions weren't really right for an avalanche and, well—" she breathed a long sigh, Track feeling the rising and falling of her breasts against his chest "—the telephone lines, the Telex are out. And the avalanche couldn't possibly have caused that. I bought a helicopter a few months ago—did I tell you?" She looked up, her face etched with a forced smile.

"No, you didn't tell me."

"We have a radio, but it's for contacting the helicopter and for the helicopter to contact the house. Unfortunately, the helicopter is in Zurich—some mechanical problem—Zulu would know about it. But the radio isn't really any good for anything else."

"So, we're cut off," Track murmured, stating the obvious more succinctly than it had already been stated. "And we're under siege."

"Yes," she whispered.

"Who?" Track asked, still holding her.

"The funny thing—" she laughed, a soft, almost little-girl-sounding laugh "—is that even in the old days, I wouldn't do business with the Libyans—they always seemed like such positive asses. But this Captain Sadek Mohammed—at least that's what he calls himself—was persistent. There were little devices that a Bulgarian had invented to jam AWACs radar. Well, Zulu and I arranged to steal one and the plans. The Russians got mad and had the East Germans kill the Bulgarian, and Sadek wanted the device. Since nobody else in the world had it, the plans, or knew how it worked, he came to me. I wouldn't sell it to him. I sold it to the Americans. But I kept a duplicate set of the plans in my vault in Zurich, just in case."

"And now Sadek wants to kill you?"

She looked up at him. He noticed she was biting her lower lip. "Um-hmm."

"Why can't we ski out?"

"The only way is through a rather narrow pass. Sadek would have that blocked. One man could stop a dozen men if he knew what he was doing."

"And Sadek's man would know what he was doing, wouldn't he?"

"There was a rumor that Sadek helped to plan

the attack on the base of your American Marines in Beirut. He. . . he is very—"

Somehow, as Dan Track held her tightly against him, he could understand why she hadn't used the word "good."

9

Sadek Mohammed had experienced snow for the very first time while a student at Patrice Lumumba University. And in many ways he had found it little different than sand. When snow filled the air, as it did now in the higher elevations, it could obscure one from one's enemies. And like sand blown on the wind, snow, too, could form obstacles. But snow's mass was more controllable to be engineered for destruction. The avalanche his men had started under his direction would close the road for at least another day.

Sadek Mohammed smiled. Like the desert and its sand, these mountains would conceal his movements until the very last second. Rather than the desert khakis he had worn so often on so many other battlefields, he wore a white snow smock and white pants covering his ski clothes. The snow smock itself had a white hood, and to protect the lower portion of his face beneath his white-framed snow goggles, he wore a white silk scarf tied bandit fashion.

Whiteness—he remembered the color of Desiree

Goth's skin. He would see all of it at his leisure before he disemboweled her with his knife.

"Captain, all is in readiness," said one of his men, disturbing his thoughts.

"Then may Allah guide our hands and confuse the vision of our enemies," Sadek told his subordinate. The man was panting in the rarified atmosphere, and Sadek looked at him, listened to his breathing, watched the clouds of steam rise with the movements of his lips, the quivering of his nostrils.

"Tonight, Mademoiselle Goth shall learn what truly she has sold all these many years—death," said Sadek, laughing.

10

It was the first time Dan Track had seen Desiree's "private stock"—the vault room beyond the gymnasium area beneath the first floor. Zulu had fiddled with the combination locks on the vault door, and now, with the door swung open, Desiree led him inside.

"My God," Track murmured.

"Just a few things put away for the proverbial rainy day, Major," Zulu said, his voice resonating from behind Track.

"Yeah—sure." Track nodded, looking past Desiree.

At the end of the vault, he saw ten Steyr-Mannlicher SSG countersniping rifles, and from the distance the scopes all looked to be from Kahles.

Below these were ten SPAS-12 shotguns, the same version as the SPAS he himself carried regularly. He glanced at Desiree and she smiled, whispering, "I wanted you to feel at home."

He nodded, continuing his mental inventory of the arms room: M-16s, Uzi submachine guns,

Mini-Uzis, Walther MPKs and Remington police pumps hung, stood and lay on their sides in impressive array. Backing these up was a collection that contained multiple examples of just about every important tactical rifle, SMG and handgun to be found in the European arsenal. Track felt like a kid in a candy store.

"I'm afraid that we have never stocked revolvers for defensive use, Major," Zulu said. "So you will look in vain for a Smith & Wesson .357."

But Track was already moving for what he knew he'd need—a SPAS-12, a Walther MPK and the P-5.

Zulu walked across the vault room toward a steel cabinet, unlocked it and removed something Track immediately recognized. A Hawk MM-1 40mm revolving-cylinder grenade launcher. "I won't use this," Zulu began, turning around, "unless the dire necessity of the moment should dictate it. Grenades do so much damage."

"Right," Track said. "You wouldn't want to offend the gardener. Got anything else that might scar the earth in there?"

"Another of these, but I suspect one will prove adequate to the task," Zulu answered soberly. "I should recommend, Miss Desiree," the big black continued, "that you and the servants would be well advised to post yourselves near the vault room. At the slightest indication the house has been penetrated, you could withdraw, closing the vault behind you. I feel confident they would find the vault door impregnable and the vault—'' Zulu looked at Track now ''—is of course fireproof to a temperature of—''

''No,'' Desiree whispered. ''You're talking about me hiding away. I can fight as well as either of you—or nearly as well,'' she added.

''I am indeed aware of the full range of your considerable abilities, Miss Desiree, and it was not my suggestion that you hide, but rather that you assume the rear-guard function. Major Track can man the electronic intruder-defense-monitoring systems and at the same time guard the upper floors of the residence. I feel I may best serve by secreting myself about the grounds and taking the advantage of what element of surprise may be—''

''Bullshit,'' Track interrupted. ''I knew it.'' Track hammered his fist on the table, a neat stack of M-16 magazines toppling. ''One of those latent self-sacrificing heroes—I always had you pegged that way. Desiree can monitor the security stuff until we engage the enemy, then get down here and lock herself in with the servants until we mop up these assholes. You and I'll both be out there playing cowboys and Indians.''

''I will not lock myself in the vault and hide from the fighting, but I agree the household staff—''

Track interrupted Desiree. ''Promise me that when you hear the first shot, you'll get in here and lock the door behind you. Otherwise, so help me, I'll clip you on the jaw right now and lock you in myself."

"You wouldn't hit me—yes, you would!"

Track leaned toward her, kissing her forehead, smiling as he leaned away. "All right," Desiree continued. "But only after the fighting starts—and I'll be armed."

"Of course you'll be armed, Miss Desiree," Zulu added.

Desiree looked at Track, then at Zulu, her blue eyes flashing. "Men!" she exclaimed, and picking up an M-16 and an Uzi, she stormed from the vault.

Track turned to Zulu, still hearing the clicking of Desiree's boots against the hard surface of the floor. "Congratulations, Major," the big man said as he smiled, flashing his large white teeth.

"And congratulations to you, Zulu," Track added, nodding.

"I must confess," Zulu said, picking up a folding-stock Remington 870 shotgun, an Uzi and an M-16 already slung to his body, "that occasionally of late I find myself marginally tolerating you. Curious—perhaps a function of time."

"The more you know me the more you figure I'm not such a bad guy?"

Zulu shook his head gravely. "Rather, I fear, a function of increasing age. As time mellows one, there seems a natural tendency to dismiss the more trivial annoyances."

"Fuck you," Track told him flatly, picking up the Walther MPK. A Norwegian engineer's bag and the SPAS were already slung on his body.

The massive black man raised his eyebrows slightly, then turned and started out of the vault. Track followed him, saying, "When I retire, I'm going to write an exercise book. Call it *Arm Yourself for Fitness*—what do you think?"

Zulu didn't answer him.

11

Sergei Baslovitch eased his right heel against the Volvo's brake pedal, the toe of his black loafer working the gas pedal simultaneously as his left foot pumped the clutch, double-clutching to downshift before reaching the police roadblock. His mouth was momentarily dry—a natural reaction, he realized. Despite Swiss neutrality, Switzerland was still the West and Soviet-Swiss relations were not always cordial. After a second's consideration, Baslovitch dismissed the idea that the roadblock had anything to do with him. With the skis mounted in the roof rack, he could be any tourist. His gun and the other accessories he had requested of the head of the Zurich Station were securely hidden behind the driver's door panel.

As the Volvo was pulling to a halt, a smiling Swiss policeman, carrying a flashlight and wearing a holstered pistol at his side, was already walking toward the car. The name on Baslovitch's Austrian passport read Heinrich Schuler. Accenting his voice with his most lilting German, he took the impetus from the police officer, shouting to the man as the car finally stopped on the snow-packed roadbed, "What's blocking the road?"

"An avalanche, sir—no traffic can get through."

"But I must return to Austria!"

"Another route, then, sir—the avalanche has completely closed the road. Not even a bicycle could get through." The policeman gestured into the distance with his flashlight and smiled.

Baslovitch forced himself to laugh. "Then I suppose I will need to find myself a warm bed somewhere for the night."

"I envy you. I must stay here and warn travelers away. You'll have to turn here, sir—this is the only place wide enough."

Baslovitch nodded, bidding the policeman goodnight and promising to have a drink for him with the first pretty girl he found. "Why not," he said to himself as he found reverse and backed up the Volvo.

Baslovitch shifted into first, popped the clutch and hit the Volvo's horn, giving the policeman a wave through the open window.

Baslovitch licked his lips. A coincidence? A sudden avalanche blocks the only access to the home of Desiree Goth, and his latest intelligence data reveals Dan Track is now at Desiree Goth's house.

There had to be something wrong—because coincidence did not exist.

THE SKI BOOTS were not a bad fit, but not good, either. Baslovitch smiled, locking his left boot into its breakaway binding, then locking in his right. He had changed to ski clothes, leaving his Austrian-businessman garb under a blanket on the back seat.

His silk glove liners already in place, his leather ski mittens hanging beneath his jacket's storm cuffs, Baslovitch lifted the P-7 from the driver's seat, the interior door panel already clipped back into place. He cycled the top round off the magazine into the chamber, securing the P-7 into the special pocket built into the lining of his jacket just beneath his left armpit. Two spare magazines disappeared into pouches on the right side of the jacket, and a third went into a pocket on the bib front of his bright blue ski pants.

Baslovitch slammed the door of the Volvo, and thrust his hands inside the mittens.

He picked up his ski poles. He would be glad to be moving because the cold was beginning to numb him. The topographical map—provided it was correct and the snow conditions were as he anticipated—seemed to him to indicate a run of not much more than an hour.

Baslovitch settled the poles in his fists as he eased away from the Volvo, wondering what lay ahead in the night, between him and Dan Track.

12

Track could feel the warmth of Desiree's voice as it hummed in his left ear through the radio set. "You are sure Zulu can't hear us?" he said into the handset.

"His set's only got one frequency—yours has two," Desiree replied. "If I hear him calling you I can tell you to switch off and turn to his frequency."

"So, how ya doin'?"

"Fine. Have I ever told you that sometimes I want to marry you?"

"Why just sometimes?" Track whispered into the radio.

"You have your work, I have mine. And I don't think the Consortium particularly likes me, anyway."

"After what you did to save the President from Krieger's men, they should."

"I just love you. So very much."

"Why am I out here in the cold?" Track asked her, snow falling now in large flakes around him, settling on the backs of his hands. His left hand held the radio near his lips, his right hand was bunched around the pistol grip of the SPAS-12. "Why am I out in the cold, then?" Track said again. "We should be back beside that fireplace."

"I'm sorry I got you involved in my troubles, Dan. I—" The radio went silent.

"Hey, look—your troubles are my troubles, kid. Pretty soon Zulu and I will have polished off these creeps and everything will be okay." He let up the talk button. No voice came over the static-filled speaker. "Desiree? I've lost you—come back."

Then her voice crackled in his ear. "Switch frequencies, Dan."

"Hell," Track muttered, turning the selector on the body of the radio to the frequency shared with Zulu.

He could hear Zulu's voice. "The front wall, you say, Miss Desiree?"

"Yes, six of them that I could count. And the power here in the house is gone—the generator kicked on so quickly the lights only flickered. But all the alarms were set off during the power interruption and so they're useless."

Track spoke into his set. "You take the servants and get down by the vault—now! Be ready to swing that vault door shut fast. Track out."

"Please, both of you, don't get killed," Desiree said in a pleading voice before adding, "Desiree out."

Track spoke into the handset. "Zulu—just like we planned it, right?"

"Agreed. Zulu out—and good luck."

"The same, Cuddles." Track rammed the radio set back into its pouch on the left side of his belt. With all the guns and ammo, he felt like a pack animal. But he started to run....

ZULU FOUGHT from a fixed position. He sat now, in the trees beside the road and two hundred yards from the main gate, in the lotus position, all his senses focused on the night, the M-16 across his thighs, his clothes blacker than his skin.

He was not a Zulu—the tribe of fierce African warriors. His was a different tribe, despite the name Desiree had given him. His expression intensified as he recalled his jungle life, and remembered the little girl named Desiree he had found wandering alone in the jungle, terrified by the rogue mercenaries and the insanely homicidal brother who had pursued her.

There was a story told about the fire when he was a boy, a story of twelve men from his tribe who had given their lives in battle. The warriors had been away, pursuing their enemy, and the only males left in the village were the boys not yet old enough to be warriors, and the men past the age of being warriors. These were the historic twelve defenders. One among them—very old, the grandfather of the youngest boy, who was only eleven—had traveled far from his homeland. Rather than fight with spear or bow he fought with a long knife. Zulu could see the man in his mind, wielding some impossibly huge sword from some long-gone epoch.

The enemy had come, and the women and children had taken flight deeper into the jungle while a young runner pursued the village warriors to get them to return. The young runner, as the tale went, died when his heart burst in his chest. But he found the warriors, blood spilling from his lips as he told them of the evil that had taken place.

The warriors returned, but there was no battle.

The one hundred warriors of the enemy were all slain.

The twelve defenders—the very young and the very old—were also dead. The legend told of the returning warriors finding the old grandfather who had traveled to the far-off lands and fought with the strange long knife. The old man was dead—one clean wound through the heart from a spear thrust but his clothing, his body, his face were drenched in the blood of his enemies.

Draped across him was the body of the youngest defender, the eleven-year-old boy. The boy's hands still clutched the fabled long knife, the steel gleaming with blood. Like the grandfather, a single spear thrust to the heart had killed him.

The grandfather's body was buried—the custom of Zulu's people through the ages—and the boy's body was buried beside him. Both men were given warrior funerals.

But not even the strongest man in the village had been able to pry the boy's fingers from the hilt of the sword, and the long knife of the legend was buried with him, clutched as firmly in death as in life.

The tale of the twelve defenders had been a favorite story with every boy in his village, and Zulu smiled, thinking of it. Like other boys, he would fashion for himself something that matched his mental picture of the long knife, and would fantasize himself going to his death with courage in the defense of his loved ones.

His real family was dead, slaughtered during the Congo Civil War. Now, Desiree Goth was his family. He felt at once like a brother, like a father, seeing in her deeper friendship than he would have thought could exist between two people so different.

It was why he tolerated the American, Dan Track, he supposed—because Desiree Goth loved him. And because of that, he would continue to try to understand the ex-Army CID major, the man whose personnel data indicated an IQ well into the genius range, yet who talked like someone raised on the streets.

Another type of jungle, Zulu thought. Another type of war.

A sound brought his subconscious attention

back to the level of the conscious. To clear the mind one had to use the mind. He had used memory to sharpen his perception of reality.

He heard the sound again.

He remained in the lotus position, not moving his hands, his rifle, his body in any way.

He thought of the man-boy in the legend of the twelve defenders. None of his weapons even remotely resembled the long knife. But the sword the boy had not surrendered even in death was not the point of the legend.

Zulu knew that well.

The enemy was coming.

Coming.

The snow fell, the flakes almost warm against what little exposed skin remained from the black navy watch cap pulled low over his ears, the black woolen turtleneck that rose nearly to his chin, the black leather gloves that nearly met the cuffs of his sweater.

He moved his toes inside his black combat boots, feeling the sensation in his legs.

He moved his fingers, feeling the sensation in his arms.

He was a warrior, and the thought amused him. The tradition of the twelve defenders was part of his blood.

A flicker of movement and in one swift motion he rose to his full height. Deep in the shadow of the trees, the blackness hid him.

The M-16 shifted in his hands, and his thumb found the safety, moving it with an audible click to full-auto.

The click would be warning enough that honor be served against another warrior. If the men invading the retreat of Desiree Goth, which he would defend with his life and his soul if necessary, had not heard the sound of the safety tumbler moving, then they were not warriors and deserved no respect.

He fired the M-16, killing three men in one long burst before they could turn to face him fully. Their bodies bounced back, blood spurting from severed arteries, coloring the white of their snow smocks, the white of the snow.

Warrior.

Another of the invaders appeared. Desiree had been wrong—there were more than six. There were many. Zulu fired, killing the man, the body lurching, twisting, pirouetting, a scream issuing from the twisted lips, a submachine gun blazing into the night sky.

Zulu fired the M-16 at another man, the man's body doubling forward, rolling, bouncing, slamming hard against a tree trunk and stopping.

Zulu opened his hands and the M-16 fell to the snow beside him. His right fist found the Uzi, and his left hand worked the bolt open. His finger moved against the trigger—three more of the white-clad men went down.

Silence. Zulu stood, in his heart wanting to free one of the last three men who struggled now uselessly against death, his torso ripped and shredded from the full metal case 9mms of the submachine gun.

Then he moved deeper into the shadow, leaving the M-16 where it lay—a lost weapon meant a weakened adversary and it would buy him their carelessness.

The man finally died. Zulu did not close his eyes as he watched.

The Uzi was his sword as he held it clasped tight in his fists—as the man-boy, last of the twelve defenders, had held his long knife.

Zulu waited.

13

Baslovitch climbed uphill, the inside edges of his skis biting deep into the fresh snow. Knees bent, weight forward, his poles dug in, he felt every sense reaching out into the night. The pass would be at the base of the hill on the other side. And if the avalanche were for some reason beyond the whim of nature, then someone would be guarding access to the area. The logical place for that would be at the narrow confines of the pass.

He stopped making his herringbone pattern when his head was just below the crest of the ridge. He would be vulnerable, but there was no preventing that without taking perhaps twelve hours to circle the pass.

Baslovitch reached inside his ski jacket and withdrew his Heckler & Koch P-7, jacking back the slide. His ski mittens were stuffed under his armpit, and only the silk glove liners protected his hands against the cold that engulfed him. When he had stopped at the base of the hill, he had unclipped the mittens from the bindings across his shoulders under his jacket. If he had to fire, he wanted nothing dangling from his cuffs that would get in the way. He returned the P-7 to its integral holster, securing the right-hand mitten in an outside pocket, zipping the pocket shut.

He pulled the other mitten back in place.

He left the front of his jacket zipped halfway down from his throat, despite the cold.

Baslovitch grasped his poles, his right hand already stinging with the cold, the tips of his fingers slightly numb.

He sidestepped a short way up the hill, keeping his frame bent, his profile as low as possible. Less than four feet below the crest, Baslovitch dug in his poles, twisting his body up and left, his knees rising, his legs tucking under him and hurtled his weight forward and to the left.

Baslovitch was up, moving now, digging his poles in as he slipped across the crest of the hill. He was moving rapidly down, his body low, both poles moving as he adjusted his angle along the slope. His body was like a thread penetrating the needle eye of the narrow snow-covered pass situated halfway down the hill and below him.

His body was slicing through the air, the cold tearing at him. He shifted his right pole to his left hand, the left hand rising, tucking both ski poles beneath the left arm to trim his silhouette. His right hand grasped the butt of the P-7 inside his jacket.

Faster—the pass was ahead. He was thinking in English and he hoped it wasn't "dead" ahead.

Suddenly, he detected movement near the mouth of the pass on the right of the rise.

His right hand jerked from beneath the blue ski jacket as he saw a man silhouetted against the snow and the flash of assault-rifle fire. Baslovitch knew the sound too well, it was an AKM. The gun had been supplied by his own country. *"Merde,"* he snapped, his body already rolling in the snow. If an avalanche was possible, the gunshots could start it.

His breakaway bindings had worked, and with his feet clear of the skis he wriggled across the snow. Getting footing, he threw himself into a low run as the snow near his feet ripped in upward-thrusting wedges and more gunfire roared.

Baslovitch threw himself down beside a large mogul that offered no cover but some concealment. His right fist tightened on the P-7, activating the squeeze cocker, and he triggered a rapid two-round semiautomatic burst toward the rifleman. The rifleman's body seemed to twitch with it, but the mogul exploded with another burst of AK fire. Baslovitch was up and moving again, firing as he ran, pinning the rifleman down. Baslovitch hurtled forward over a small drift, rolling down into what in snowless weather would be some sort of ditch. Snow sifted down the collar of his turtleneck and clung to his face.

Two rounds were left in the P-7, and Baslovitch saw an opportunity to use an old diversion. Quickly he snapped the P-7 over the rise and fired the two rounds, then ducked.

Return gunfire ripped into the snowbank as he worked the slide stop down, the P-7 cocking again but over an empty chamber. Baslovitch pulled the trigger, hoping the click would be audible.

It sounded loud in the winter stillness.

He extracted the spent magazine, and rammed a fresh one into the butt. Then he took the empty magazine and pitched it into the snow, hoping the rifleman would mistake it for his pistol.

He muffled the pistol with his body, bending low over it, and slowly drew back the slide, letting it run forward as silently as he could.

"I'm hurt," he shouted in German. Then again in English, "I'm hurt. Who are you?"

There was no answer. "Look, I'm just trying to cross the pass. Please don't shoot."

Already Baslovitch was edging along the length of the embankment, getting closer to the side of the pass where the rifleman had been positioned.

Another burst of gunfire from the AKM ripped down into the embankment—the gunman would be standing now, Baslovitch reasoned.

He kept moving, crawling on knees and elbows along the embankment, cutting the distance.

He would have only one chance.

Another burst of AKM fire. The magazine should be nearly empty if the gunner had not already changed it, Baslovitch thought. The bullets came into the snow packed ditch at a deeper angle; it meant that the rifleman was standing higher.

Baslovitch pushed himself up and stood, the P-7 in both fists. He lined up the sights on the man seventy-five yards away, catching him changing sticks for the AKM.

Baslovitch could see the man's face—Arab.

He had a number of good friends who were Arabs, but this fellow wasn't going to be one of them, Baslovitch decided. He triggered a 2-round burst, bringing the muzzle back on line, then another 2-round burst, sending the Arab's body rocking.

The body slipped from sight, the AK going with it.

Baslovitch quickly ducked, ejected the partially empty magazine and pushed a fresh one into the butt. He let the slide go forward, and peered over the embankment.

There was no movement.

Baslovitch pushed himself up and rolled over the embankment. He went into a dead run toward the pass, throwing himself against one of its sheer walls. Chunks of snow fell around his shoulders.

Cautiously he edged around a corner, and eased along a face of snow-encrusted rock. Then he stopped.

Baslovitch drew a deep breath and threw himself past the edge of the wall. He rolled, the pistol in his right fist.

Just as suddenly, he eased his grip, letting the P-7 decock.

He recognized death when he saw it, and he saw it on the blood-stained body in the smile that was the rictus of death.

14

Dan Track lay flat on the snow-covered ground, watching the feet of two of the invaders as they passed on the far side of the pine trees behind which he hid. The last of the two men passed him, and Track reached out as he threw himself up and between the trees, his hand ripping the drag man's foot from beneath him, pitching the man down into the snow.

Track wheeled to the right, his foot snaking out in a double tae kwon-do kick to the chest of the lead man as the man spun toward him. Track finished the turn, thrusting his weight upward, his right foot hammering into the man's neck, crushing his Adam's apple.

Turning, Track caught sight of the drag man kneeling, bringing his AKM to bear. Track's left foot snapped out, and the heel of his boot crushed the man's nose. Even as he rocked back, his eyes wide, arms flung away from the sides of the body, the man was dead, his ethmoid bone spiking into his brain.

Sensing more of the invaders coming from his

right, Track dodged back into the cover of the trees as subgun fire hammered toward him. Track hit the snow in a roll, and came up with the Walther MPK in both fists, spraying lead toward the advancing terrorists. Two more went down, dead or soon to be dead. The others scrambled for cover.

But Track was up and running again, letting the Walther fall to his side, bringing up the SPAS. More men rushed over the wall to his right—this wasn't a light penetration for a hit against Desiree, he thought, it was a small army.

Dan Track fired the SPAS-12, spraying buckshot toward the terrorists dropping over the wall. Men crashed to the snow, shrieking with pain as Track peppered the wall with pellets, shredding flesh and bone.

The SPAS was out and with no time to reload, Track let it fall to his side. Assault-rifle and subgun fire tore into the snow and earth, snagged at the tree trunks, sent bark flying amid the metal-jacketed lead in a maelstrom around him.

As he was running, bringing the MPK up, he heard a voice shout, "Major—down!"

"Desiree," Track rasped, throwing himself to the snow as subgun fire laced the air over his head. Zulu's Uzi chattered in response.

Terrorists were going down.

Track worked the trigger of the MPK in neat bursts. The roar of Zulu's Uzi stopped, then thunder began as Zulu brought up the Remington 870 shotgun. Track heard the boom, the *chunk-chunk* sound of the pump tromboning, the boom again, then the *chunk-chunk* sound.

Track saw the last muzzle-flash of the shotgun, then ran toward it, seeing Zulu backlit by the house lights for an instant, then seeing something huge and unworldly gleaming in the man's hands.

It was the Hawk MM-1 40mm grenade launcher.

"Look out, Major! The gardener will never forgive me," Zulu shouted as he stepped from the trees, the Hawk beside his hip. Track threw himself onto his back and heard the roar, the whistle, then the blast. The cluster of trees near the wall were suddenly consumed in a mushroom-shaped orange-and-yellow fireball, whole chunks of trees and human torsos flew skyward, then crashed to earth. Zulu fired the Hawk again and again.

Track reloaded the MPK, and as some of the terrorists ran from the trees, their bodies aflame like living torches he fired into them, cutting the men down.

He glanced to his right. The lights in the main house were out. With Zulu still hanging out with the Hawk, Track leaped up and ran toward the house. Throwing down the MPK, the magazine spent, he ripped the SPAS from his shoulders and rammed fresh double-O buck loads into the magazine tube.

The SPAS loaded, Track worked the magazine cutoff button, cramming the ninth round into the chamber, then letting the bolt slide home.

"Desiree!" He screamed the name into the night. The darkened house could mean only one thing. The enemy was inside and had cut off the emergency generator.

"Desiree!"

A hundred yards from the house, Track saw some of the invaders coming down the three front steps leading from the porch. Track unleashed the SPAS, and the bodies of the four men danced in the darkness as the air was filled with startled screams and splinters of wood and stone.

He was at the driveway now, and assault-rifle fire hammered down toward him from the roof. He snarled, hitting the gravel, rolling, bringing the SPAS up and firing toward the roof line. There was another muzzle-flash, and Track felt something tearing at his right thigh, like a slash with the blade of a hot knife. He fired the SPAS, spraying the nearest end of the roof. There was another blast of AKM fire, then a body toppled from the eaves. Track was up, moving, reloading the SPAS as the body hit.

Track's hand swiped at his thigh as he hit the steps—his fingers came away wet with blood. But he felt no pain as he ran, taking the steps in a single jump.

He wheeled right on his injured leg, and suddenly the pain ripped through him. He kicked at the door lock with his left foot and the door shot open. Track lurched into the house, hitting the hallway in a forward roll as gunfire hammered through the door and into the wall near him. Track fired at a shadow at the head of the steps, the SPAS recoiling as he emptied half the magazine. A lone gunman pitched forward and tumbled down the steps.

As the body slammed to a stop at the base of the stairs, Track was already moving. Pausing for an instant, he snapped his left foot to the base of the man's skull, delivering a final blow.

Recharging the SPAS's magazine, Track neared the stairs leading to the weapons vault. If only Desiree had listened, he thought.

There was a scream, more anger than anguish.

"Desiree," Track shouted. He knew he was being a fool, but he took the stairs to the lower level three at a time in a dead run.

He hit the base of the stairs, ready to die but determined to take every one of them with him. What he saw chilled him.

"Dan—don't. He'll kill Sarah!"

The voice was Desiree's, and less than a yard from her, near the pool, stood an Arab, the man's arm binding Sarah, Desiree's maid, against him. His other hand held a Gurkha knife, with the edge pressed against the maid's throat. Beside Desiree stood another man, tall, gaunt looking. From the cut of his web gear and the weapons festooned on him, the man was obviously the leader. Other men holding high-intensity flashlights surrounded them, lighting up the otherwise blackened gym.

And then Track saw the knife the gaunt man held pressed against Desiree's side.

"You must be the American since you are not big enough or dark enough to be the African," the gaunt man intoned.

"Perceptive of you," Track whispered hoarsely.

"You should, I think, drop your weapons to the floor."

"Why? So you can kill Desiree?"

Track's eyes flickered around the room. He counted six men, but perhaps more were out of sight in some other portion of the lower level, hiding in the shadows. The butler was down on the floor, a trickle of blood coming from his left temple, the whole left side of his face purpling with a bruise. The cook, Elvira, was huddled in the far corner, beyond the pool. A man with an AKM stood over her.

"Yes, so I can kill Mademoiselle Goth. But there is no need to kill these others or yourself."

"Yeah, well, that's sweet of you," Track told him, stalling, his mind calculating the best of the bad odds. "But I've killed a lot of your men already, and you don't look like the type to forgive that. And Zulu's taken out so many of your guys it isn't funny. Anyway, Zulu's on his way. Don't let all that Oxford polish fool you—he's a killing machine. Efficient like you wouldn't believe. Naw, I don't think you'd let us live. And besides, if you kill Desiree, I'm gonna do worse than kill you. Takes a real chicken shit to hold a knife on a woman—pretty typical for you Libyan military assholes." And Dan Track licked his lips, watching the gaunt man's eyes. "You wouldn't have the guts to try killing me with a knife. An unarmed woman, sure. But you don't have the balls to fight me with a knife, one on one."

What might have been a smile—Track wasn't sure—crossed the Libyan leader's face. Then the Libyan said, "Give him a knife—unless, of course, he has one already."

"Matter of fact," Track said, grinning, "I left mine at home. Tell you what, though—you use a knife. I won't need one for dog shit like you."

The Libyan stepped away. "I am Sadek Mohammed—you should know this before you die."

"I'm Dan Track—can't say it's nice to meet you."

"Put your weapons—"

"You bet. First, you let Desiree stand over by the wall, release the maid and have that turd with the AKM step back from the cook."

"Agreed." Sadek said something Track couldn't understand before shoving Desiree away from him. "Does that suit you?" Sadek said as he smiled.

"Yeah." Track felt that honor didn't bind him—if he could have swung his gun into position and started shooting without risk to Desiree or the household staff he would have. But no opportunity presented itself.

Track set down the SPAS, then drew the Walther P-5 from his belt and set it on the tile floor, as well.

He looked into Sadek's eyes a moment—the message was clear: Sadek wanted to kill him. There would be no tricks.

"All right, let's do it," Track whispered.

Track rose to his full height, weaponless, his fists flexing open and closed, not taking his eyes from the Libyan commander. His leg hurt whenever he moved it, but it still worked.

He wanted Sadek angry. As Track stopped slightly more than three feet from the Libyan, he smiled, saying, "You know, this was a real dumb play on your part. I'm so heavy in martial arts that I taught it for a while. Tae kwon-do's what I like—but I know some kung fu, some judo. And anyway, any American worth his salt could take out a dozen of you clowns with just his fists. We learn how to handle ourselves. We grow up polishing off a half dozen wimps like you each morning before breakfast."

Sadek lunged with the knife. Track estimated the double-edged blade's length as perhaps eighteen inches and the width from edge to edge close to three inches. He dodged, but not too rapidly. Sadek was feeling out his reaction patterns, his response times, his reflexes, and Track didn't want to let him know too much. Sadek lunged again, and Track dropped to his right knee, his wounded leg screaming in protest. He stuck his right hand out for balance and swept his left leg against Sadek's legs. It wasn't his best move, but he had no desire for Sadek to see that yet.

Sadek stumbled back, but didn't go down.

Track rolled out of the drop and to his feet.

Sadek was already advancing, the knife slicing the air with a sickening whistling sound as Track jumped back.

The Libyan was fast and knew it.

Track glanced to his left, toward the pool. If he could get Sadek into the pool, the natural drag would slow him down.

Sadek's knife was there again, slashing, halting, thrusting like a rapier. Track leaped back, wheeling half left, and planted a kick against Sadek's rib cage with his wounded right leg.

Sadek stumbled, losing his balance, as Track spun and kicked his left foot into Sadek's chest. Sadek backed toward the pool, and Track wheeling again, feigning a kick with his right foot as Sadek threw himself forward, hacking with the sword-sized blade. As Sadek lunged toward him, Track planted his weight on his right foot, and hammered his left fist into Sadek's jaw, feeling it as the skin on his knuckles split. Then Track shifted his balance, coming down on his left foot, his right foot kicking up into Sadek's face.

Sadek sagged back, moving his arms like a clumsy bird, trying to shift his weight and prevent a fall, his body stumbling, tumbling, into the pool. Track hurtled after the Libyan.

As Track entered the pool, Sadek's knife hacked down, missing Track's left shoulder by inches. Track countered by thrusting himself out of the water, his right fist breaking the surface and smashing into the base of Sadek's chin, snapping the head back.

As Track dove beneath the surface, he could see Sadek arcing the knife. Track's left hand snaked out, blocking the right arm of his opponent for an instant, and his right hand thrust forward under the water's surface, gouging at Sadek's testicles, ripping them forward. The Libyan shrieked with pain, and Track rammed his fist into the bridge of Sadek's nose. The pool was suddenly red with the blood gushing from the Libyan's nostrils.

Then Sadek screamed. "Shoot him! Shoot him now!"

Track's right fist hammered upward, thrusting out of the water, ramming into Sadek's jaw. Sadek's body rose out of the water, the back arching.

Gunfire echoed off the walls of the pool enclosure, and Track dived beneath the surface of the water, stroking his body downward and across to the far edge of the pool. In his left hand he held Sadek's short sword.

As Track rose out of the water, bullets stitched the surface where he had been, and burrowed into Sadek's chest.

Track shifted the giant knife to his right hand and threw, the blade impaling the nearest of the five remaining Libyans square in the chest, riveting the man to the tiled wall.

Track was up, out of the water, sprinting toward the far side of the pool.

Shotgun fire filled the air, and Track turned to see Zulu, a riot shotgun in hands, pumping out death. One of Sadek's men took two hits and vaulted backward into the pool, slamming against Sadek's body.

And beside Zulu, an Uzi spitting fire in his hands, stood Sergei Baslovitch.

15

Since he was wet already, it fell to Dan Track to go into the bloodied waters of the swimming pool and tow the bodies close enough to the edge for Zulu and Baslovitch to lift them out.

Desiree had left the pool area after Zulu had restored power to the house, taking her staff with her.

"There are many bodies outside," Sergei Baslovitch remarked. "We have our work cut out for us."

"Why are you here?" Track asked the Russian, pushing the bloodied and sodden corpse of Sadek Mohammed out of the swimming pool.

"I'll tell you later, Dan," the Russian said, glancing toward Zulu.

Track wiped the bloodied water from his face as it dripped from his hair. "Much as I hate to say it, I don't really think I need to keep anything from Zulu. What you can tell me later you can tell me now."

Track watched Baslovitch as the KGB major shrugged. "Very well. If that is the case, I'll wait until we are through with the bodies and tell you in front of Miss Goth as well. I have no desire to repeat this—it is too complicated."

"All right," Track said, pulling himself up against the edge of the pool and climbing out of the water. "We'll wait until then."

Zulu cleared his throat. "Major Baslovitch, since Major Track is all wet...." And Zulu paused for what Track interpreted as dramatic effect.

"I like you, too, Zulu," Track said.

"I propose that the two of us handle the bodies outside the house. We have two large vans with which to transport them to the storage area beyond the garage. Such storage should serve admirably until more permanent arrangements can be made."

Baslovitch let out a long sigh. Track guessed the Russian was tired. "Why not?" Baslovitch responded. The KGB major reslung the Uzi he had taken from a dead terrorist, adding, "In case they aren't all quite dead."

"Great," Track said. "I'll grab a shower and maybe Desiree can get the cook to rustle up some food."

"Miss Desiree has already indicated that she would personally prepare some delicacy for our consumption—a rare treat awaits us all," Zulu stressed, picking up his shotgun.

"How rare?" Track asked, but Zulu either

didn't hear or ignored him, as he started up the stairs toward the main floor. Baslovitch followed him.

Track looked down at the body of Sadek Mohammed.

Dan Track just shook his head, stepped over the body and walked away.

TRACK STOOD under the hot shower, washing the blood of his enemies from his body and hair. He had removed an imbedded rock chip from his right leg, and he winced as the hot water entered the wound. Despite the battle with Sadek and his killers, Track's thoughts were all directed toward another matter. Baslovitch. What was the Russian doing here? Track turned the water to straight cold and stood under it, then wondered if that had been a good idea as he shivered. After a moment his body adjusted to the drastic change and the water no longer affected him.

He stared at the crystal of the Rolex Sea-Dweller, smudging away water and studying the time. After midnight.

"Wonderful," he groaned, turning off the water, stepping out of the shower and beginning to towel down.

When he finished dressing, he found a box of gauze and some surgical tape.

There was a long night still ahead of him.

Dressed finally in comfortably fitting gray

slacks, a pale blue long-sleeved shirt and navy blue long-sleeved V-neck sweater, Track started from his rooms—but not before picking up the Walther P-5 and dropping the pistol in his hip pocket. There were spare magazines still in the credenza near the front door. He wondered if something could be done about the front door, or would they all freeze that night?

As he reached the base of the stairs, his misgivings were resolved—Zulu was standing beside the front door, holding a hammer, a tool box on the floor beside him.

The giant African turned around, as though Track had announced himself. "The repairs to the door should suffice until workmen can be summoned in the morning. Unfortunately someone destroyed the locking mechanism with what appears to have been a martial-arts kick. I wonder who?"

"Got me." Track grinned.

"No matter—the door can be braced and I plan to sit up through the morning hours and relax with a good book." It was then that Track noticed the P-5 in the waistband of Zulu's trousers. "Only one window was broken and I've repaired temporarily."

"Where's Baslovitch?" Track asked.

"Changing. Rather gritty work, I'm afraid. Blood from our dead enemies was unavoidable."

"If I were you," Track told Zulu, "I'd send the

nearest Libyan embassy a dry-cleaning bill and a nasty note."

"I shall do more than that to our Libyan friends—trust that." Zulu smiled very fleetingly, gesturing toward the rear of the main floor. "Miss Desiree awaits."

Track nodded, shrugging, then turned and walked toward the rear of the house. He could smell something cooking and it smelled good.

Track entered the huge, country-style kitchen from a long, comparatively narrow hall. The flagstone wall opposite the hall was dominated by a massive hearth that looked as though it could comfortably cook something as large as a wild boar. Blackened skillets, pots and pans hung on both sides of it and above. A fire was raging in it now.

To his right, Desiree stood in front of a large, restaurant-style stove. "You look very domestic," he said to her. She turned toward him, holding a frying pan in her right hand. "And very pretty," he added.

Track walked toward her, past the long table flanked by benches, to stand behind her.

He looked past her bared shoulders, past her cascading black hair, watching the stove and what she cooked. Sliced potatoes and onions were frying in a skillet. "I thought something simple and hearty might be nice," she said, glancing quickly over her shoulder at him as he closed his hands around her slender waist. "Steaks are in the broiler, and I'll fry the eggs while they finish. You can pour yourself a drink—I'd get it for you but my hands are full."

"So are mine," Track whispered.

He listened to her as she laughed, watched her eyes as they flickered toward him over her shoulder, then away. "I took a pie out of the freezer. I rarely have the time to bake, so when I do, I put away quite a bit. Apple pie—I hope you like it. It'll be ready just about the time we're through with the main course."

"I didn't know you could cook."

"In four years," she whispered, so low he could barely hear her over the sizzling of the potatoes in the pan, "there's still a lot you don't know about me. I like to keep some surprises."

"Hmm," Track murmured, bending over her, kissing her neck, then her ear. She squirmed out of his hands for an instant, turned toward him and put her arms around his neck. She kissed him hard and full on the lips, then just as quickly turned away. "I know—fix myself a drink," he said to her. "You want one?"

"No—but later, all right?"

Track nodded, even though she wasn't looking at him. "Where?"

"In the cupboard by the back door. If I don't have what you want in here, you can check the bar in the living room or the one in the library."

"You've got what I want in here," Track said, and he wasn't thinking about liquor. Track opened the cabinet and took down a bottle of Myers's rum. He found a glass on an adjacent cupboard, poured out three fingers, then downed half of it.

Track heard footsteps in the hallway, and setting down the glass, he reached automatically for the Walther P-5. But it was only Baslovitch. "Pour yourself a drink, Sergei—the prettiest international arms dealer in the business is making dinner."

"Anything but vodka. Sometimes the national drink doesn't satisfy." Baslovitch laughed.

"That was rough duty with the bodies—thanks for taking it," Track said.

"I could hardly say it was my pleasure. Let's see," Baslovitch said, studying the liquor cabinet. "Good Scotch—a girl I know would love this."

"Glasses are in the next cupboard over," Track said as he walked toward Desiree. He sat on a bench opposite the stove. Desiree was talking as he sipped the rum, the rum warming his stomach. "What brings you here, Major Baslovitch?"

"You two know each other?" Track asked suddenly.

"For several years," Desiree began, "although usually as competitors in Third World nations. The KGB supplies arms to many underdeveloped nations in order that they may have the basic tools of self-defense against imperialist aggression. Didn't you know?"

"Yeah, I know," Track said, laughing.

Baslovitch joined in the laughter as he sat down beside Track. On the table he placed a bottle of Scotch and a bottle of rum. "You looked potentially thirsty," Baslovitch said, nodding toward the rum.

"There's ice in the refrigerator," Desiree volunteered.

"I saw enough cold things tonight, thank you," Baslovitch replied.

As Baslovitch set his Heckler & Koch P-7 on the table, Track topped off his glass. Zulu entered the kitchen, carrying the Remington 870 riot pump casually in his left hand. As he stopped at the head of the table, he set down the shotgun, closed his eyes, inhaled deeply, then smiled, opening his eyes and saying, "As I predicted, gentlemen—a rare treat indeed!"

DAN TRACK DECIDED it was not the food but the hands that prepared it. Steak, eggs, cottage-fried potatoes, apple pie—he had eaten the same items countless times in combination but they had never quite tasted so good. Track raised his glass, Desiree seated beside him, Zulu and Baslovitch opposite them. "Gentlemen, a toast to the chef!"

"Here, here," Baslovitch added.

"Indeed," Zulu intoned, smiling.

Desiree was laughing. "It's nice to know that if I ever stop selling guns I can open a restaurant."

"I was more or less thinking of keeping your cooking to myself," Track told her. And their eyes met and she leaned toward him, kissing him lightly on the cheek, saying nothing.

After a long moment, Baslovitch cleared his throat. "I really think I ought to reveal the purpose of my coming."

Track looked at Baslovitch. "Give me a cigarette first—I don't want to ruin the smell of the food with a cigar."

Baslovitch nodded, taking a nearly full pack of Luckies from his shirt pocket. Extracting one, he passed the pack to Track, who took one for himself and one for Desiree. Track lit hers, then Baslovitch's and then his own.

"Three on a Zippo?" Zulu quipped.

"I'll watch for snipers—I promise, Zulu." Desiree laughed, a cloud of smoke issuing from her mouth and nostrils as she exhaled. "I haven't smoked one of these in years, Sergei."

"Neither have I," Track added. "Well, it was a pleasant surprise that you happened along, but why?"

"George Beegh is your only living relative, am I right?" Baslovitch began.

"Yeah," Track agreed. "His mom and dad died when he was just a teenager. His mother was my sister, Diane."

"Diane and Robert Beegh were reported dead in 1975," Baslovitch continued.

"What do you mean 'reported dead'?" Track snapped, inhaling hard on the cigarette.

"Do you remember a rather beautiful blond-haired girl from Academgorodok—Tatiana Ivanova?"

"The scientist? Sure, she's the one who figured how long we had before Krieger's bomb detonated and—"

"She met a woman whom all facts seem to indicate may well be your sister, Diane," Baslovitch said, coming directly to the point.

Dan Track dropped the cigarette from his lips and it fell to the table. He just let it burn.

TRACK STOOD in the bathroom, staring into the mirror above the sink. "Diane alive?" he whispered to his reflection.

There was a knock on the door, and then the bathroom door opened. It was Zulu.

"Miss Desiree requested that I verify your continued good health, Major."

"Yeah," Track said, licking his lips. "Yeah, tell her I'm fine. Thanks."

Zulu nodded, starting to turn away, then turned back. "Major, my mother, my father, my two sisters, my older brother and my wife all died. You have my sympathies—that someone one had thought was dead, that someone one had loved very much should perhaps be alive is most unsettling. I have never regarded you with affection, Major, and I doubt that I shall. But with Miss Desiree's consent, had I a sword, it would be at your disposal to resolve this matter, should it even require venturing beyond Soviet borders. I shall convey to Miss Desiree that you are as well as can be expected and will be joining us shortly."

Track nodded, looking away from Zulu. But before the door closed, he murmured, "Thank you."

For some reason he was compelled to stare at himself. He saw the memories, the times Diane had cried when there had been no money, no work, when George had needed food and there was none. He remembered his sister holding him as their parents had died.

His mother's last kiss. He remembered his father telling him to care for Diane if something happened and he—Dan Track—was the only man—

The bathroom door opened again, and Desiree was there. Her arms encircled him and he leaned his head against hers. "I love you," she whispered very softly.

Dan Track could feel the tightness in his throat. He could barely force the words to come, and as he said them his eyes filled with tears and her arms closed more tightly against him. "I promised my father, before he died, that. . . I promised—"

Dan Track couldn't talk anymore, and Desiree just held him.

16

By midmorning, Track had not slept. The radio had revealed that the road had been cleared of the avalanche. Zulu had contacted friends of Desiree's, and the bodies of the Libyan invaders would be retrieved and disposed of. Already the gardener and his assistant were working to restore the grounds and the damage done by Zulu's Hawk MM-1.

Track stood in the driveway, smoking one of his cigars. The sounds of carpenters repairing the door and the other damage filled the air. Baslovitch was standing beside one of Desiree's Mercedes, Zulu at the wheel to drive the Russian back to the place where his own car was parked.

"Why did you do this?" Dan Track asked, clasping Baslovitch's offered hand.

"Honor? Friendship? These words are not just confined to the West," Baslovitch said. "Insanity, perhaps—because you'll do what I would do."

"I have to."

"I know that—and very likely somehow my superiors will discover that I am responsible for you having this information and—" he grinned, raising his open palms upward and shrugging "*—c'est la guerre*, hmm?" Baslovitch smiled, bowing slightly to Desiree. She leaned up and kissed him quickly on the mouth. Baslovitch laughed. "I see why Major Track regards you so highly—not just cooking." The KGB major started to the car. As he stepped inside, through the still-open doorway he looked back, saying, "My advice—and of course if I encounter you in the Soviet Union, I shall be forced to do my duty and kill you—but my advice, Dan, is that the best route is through Afghanistan and then to Alma Ata, beyond the Hindu Kush. And bring a good sweater—reports from our troops indicate the nights get rather chilly. *Dasvadanya.*" The door slammed and the Mercedes glided across the gravel and away.

Track watched after it, hearing Desiree as she spoke. "I think he is your friend, Dan."

"Yes, you're right." He watched as the car turned out of sight beyond the trees. "Yes," he repeated.

THEY WALKED, to be alone, and Track told her virtually all he could remember about his sister.

"You will go and find the answers to your questions, won't you?" Desiree finally asked, her voice low.

Track stopped walking and looked into her blue eyes. "Isn't that what you'd do?" he asked.

"Yes," she said as she smiled. "And I'll go with you."

"No," Track countered. "And I can give you the stock line the guys in the movies always use—it's too dangerous for a woman."

"This is Switzerland," she replied, laughing. "Medical clinics perform wonders. I can always—"

Track pulled her close to him, his fingers in her hair as he held her. "No, don't do that. Besides—" he kissed her forehead "—medicine can only do so much. It would be like trying to erase the *Mona Lisa*."

"Thank you," Desiree whispered.

"But you can help me. You smuggle guns into Afghanistan, don't you? To the freedom fighters there?"

"Yes—I know the routes. I have the contacts. I can get you the men and the equipment."

"First I have to go to the States. If Diane and her husband didn't die in that crash, then I've got to know why it was staged so it looked like they did. There were two bodies, both of them burned beyond recognition. I've got to find out who set it up, find out if I'm going to be walking in on some CIA thing, or if the Russians did it—or whatever."

"Dan, what—"

"What'll I tell George? Not a damn thing. Because I don't know what I'll find. There's no sense resurrecting old ghosts for no reason. Sir Abner can think of something to keep George off my back about where I'm going."

"I'll go with you to America—I can help. I have contacts there, too—some you might not have."

"All right," Track said as he nodded. "All right. We can't get ourselves in too much trouble checking out a few things. If it does look like I'm getting too close to something, you're on the first plane out. Agreed? Otherwise I don't take you. So, are we agreed?"

"Yes, we are agreed," Desiree said, giving him a salute.

For the first time in his life, he didn't know if he trusted her answer.

17

Sir Abner Chesterton, Desiree Goth and Dan Track shared a small table in Peacock Alley on the ground floor of the Waldorf, almost directly opposite Cole Porter's piano. Sir Abner made use of a permanently rented suite at the Waldorf Astoria during the extensive periods he spent in New York City. And these days it seemed to the Englishman who served as Dan Track's liaison with the consortium of international insurance underwriters that the Park Avenue suite was indeed home. A pianist was playing "Night and Day" very easily, very softly as Sir Abner sipped his Scotch, then said, "This is a fool's errand, Dan."

"If I'd wanted somebody to state the obvious I could have told anybody," Track answered, feeling himself smile.

"But consider the options. If for some reason the Central Intelligence Agency wanted your brother-in-law and sister to appear dead, then you'll be barging in on an operation that has been under way for, loosely speaking, a decade. They shan't like that. On the other hand, if they are behind the Iron Curtain from choice, well—"

"I can't believe that. Robert was a strange guy, but not that strange."

"Then consider the third alternative, Dan—that it is a KGB-initiated undertaking. If Robert and Diane's importance was so great as to falsify their deaths and substitute two other hapless individuals in the wrecked motor car, they shall be heavily guarded indeed. And the facility your friend Major Baslovitch mentioned—mind control? Really. This is terribly hush-hush material, even in this country and my own. And the Russians are supposedly further along."

"I still don't understand," Desiree interjected as Track prepared to light her cigarette. She was beautiful, as always, and wore a low-cut black evening gown that looked like something some mythical goddess would have worn for an evening's lark in the underworld. The dress was complemented by a single black silk glove that reached well above her elbow and was bound at the wrist with a thin diamond bracelet. Her bare right hand drew the cigarette from her lips, Track noticing the imprint of her lipstick on it. "This mind-control thing," she went on. "What do they really see as a strategic advantage? I mean, I know people can use their powers of concentration to bend spoons or to predict which card will be turned out of a deck, but strategic value?"

Chesterton answered before Track could. "Remote viewing—marvelously useful for intelligence gathering, if the Russians have gotten that far along. Take this spoon-bending parlor trick—what if powers of the mind could be used to trigger a missile in a silo somewhere? Or used to track submarines when satellites fail. The Lord only knows the possibilities if the mind can be utilized as a weapon of warfare. For years, the American Navy was employing psychics to aid in tracking Soviet submarines. There have been some astounding failures, but some astounding successes, as well, my dear."

Track guillotined the tip from one of the Cuesta-Rey Six-Ts, lit it with his battered Zippo, then flicked the cowling of the lighter loudly shut. "The point is, Robert was involved in some sort of U.S. research project involving the powers of the mind. When he was off all those years while George was growing up, he was in the Himalayas, he was in Tibet—he was studying. Whatever he learned there must have been important enough for our government to hire him. And if the Russians were that much further along, that much more interested, then Robert and Diane could have been kidnapped. They could have used Diane as a permanent wedge to get Robert's cooperation in research."

"Then why did she give that girl Tatiana the story about you murdering George and trying to murder both Diane and her husband? And if she is a prisoner being used to force your brother-in-law into working for the Soviets," Desiree persisted, "then why was she off her leash at the Moscow airport?"

Before Track could answer, Chesterton spoke, his voice very low, his hands opening his silver cigarette case. Chesterton smoked so rarely, the Englishman had once told Track he frequently would throw cigarettes away because they were no longer fresh. But he lit one now, inhaling the smoke more like a wine expert would sample bouquet from some rare vintage. "There is a fourth possibility, and one not to be taken lightly. You'll recall your last major assignment—the affair in Las Vegas? The Malina terrorists were run by KGB. This could all be part of an elaborate ruse to get you on their own territory, inside the Soviet Union. And I'm not impugning this Baslovitch chap. He could be merely their innocent dupe, the KGB knowing you would trust him, knowing Baslovitch would come to you with information like this. Your sister and brother-in-law may well be in the graves you have supposed them to occupy these past ten years."

"I've thought of that. That's another reason I don't want you telling George anything. If they're dead already, I want them to stay that way."

"Tell him the rest, Dan," Desiree said. Track's eyes flickered toward her.

He nodded, letting out a long breath that sounded to him like a sigh. "All right. What if that accident they had wasn't an accident at all—whether it's them in the graves or not. Somebody's in those graves. If it wasn't an accident, somebody's gotten away with two murders for ten years now. Time that situation got rectified."

Chesterton seemed to study the glowing tip of his cigarette. "You know, when one smokes as rarely as I do, one appreciates it more. I imagine the experience is rather like the rare times the two of you spend together—sweeter for their rarity." A warm smile creased his face. "Life is a very precious thing," he continued, looking at Track. "I think that's something I like about you. I've never known of you hesitating to kill when it was necessary, nor have I known of you killing when it wasn't. You want revenge now for a real wrong or a supposed wrong, and you don't know which. Justice is one thing, vendetta another. The Chinese have a marvelous saying: when one goes seeking revenge, one should first dig two graves."

"You and I saw the same movie," Track said.

"Perhaps we did, Dan, but the wisdom of the saying stands on its own. I'll aid you in whatever ways that I can, legal or otherwise. And I gather Desiree intends to do the same. And of course I'll mislead George—but only because I value him as much as I do you, more than a co-worker, as a friend. But whatever you should find, somehow I don't think it will be to your liking."

The pianist had shifted to a livelier tune, "Anything Goes." Somehow, Track didn't think it was appropriate.

DAN TRACK did not visit George in the hospital. Instead he pressed Sir Abner Chesterton for every available detail of the younger man's recovery. And the details seemed almost miraculous. According to Chesterton, the doctors treating George had put the speed of recovery down to George's sheer physical strength and stamina. Release from the hospital, with near total recovery achieved, should be within the next two days, pending the treatment of a minor infection.

Track disliked lying, especially to someone he cared about. But he had advised Chesterton to tell George that he was still in Switzerland with Desiree and would be touring France by car with her for the next several weeks.

Chesterton had agreed.

The morning following the dinner at the Waldorf with Sir Abner, Track and Desiree had left La Guardia for Hartsfield International Airport in Atlanta. Desiree traveled with a forged passport and matching credit card and rented a car under her assumed name in the event any agency, foreign or domestic, was already interested in their plans. Taking Chesterton's advice, they had booked reservations under the names of Mr. and Mrs. Wilton Dillard. The real Wilton Dillard was one of Chesterton's lifelong friends since the days of his National Service.

Desiree drove the rented Ford LTD, while Track, familiar with Atlanta from previous trips, navigated. "Take the signs for—"

"I've been to Atlanta on business," she said, as she glanced away from the road and smiled, putting on her dark glasses against the near noonday sun.

"Sorry," Track said. "You did warn me that there were still a lot of things about you that I didn't know. So I'll ask—do you know Peter Scorese?"

"Deputy head of the domestic counterintelligence division of the CIA from 1968 until 1977," she recited. "But no, I don't know him."

"What else don't you know about him?" Track asked, cutting the tip off a cigar but not lighting it.

"Well, let's see. After leaving the CIA he started his own business—Vulcan Executive-Protection Services. The company motto is Forged in the Heat of Battle."

"But you never met him?" Track asked her.

"No. Whatever you might like to think, I usually avoid people like Peter Scorese. I'm reasonably certain he's heard of me and my business, so that was cause enough. Do you think Scorese knows anything?"

"If anybody does," Track told her, opening the flight bag he had left on the seat between them, "it would be Scorese." He removed two butterfly pistol rugs from the bag, along with a Norwegian army engineer's sack, then zipped it shut, tearing away the string that still clung to the handle from the red Firearms tag he had removed as soon as he had retrieved the bag from the luggage carousel. Track twisted in the seat, eyeing the expressway traffic. The Atlanta expressway system was the worst in the United States, he thought. The last time he had been in the city, the system had been under reconstruction and he was optimistic it would improve. As Desiree swerved to avoid a pickup truck that had apparently forgotten there wasn't an acceleration ramp, his optimism began to fade.

Stowing the flight bag on the back seat, he twisted into position beside Desiree and opened the first of the two butterfly rugs, removing an Italian-made FIE TZ-75 9mm. From the engineer's sack, he took a double-column, 15-round magazine, and rammed it into the butt of the pistol, working the slide back. Track moved the slide-mounted safety up, and the pistol was ready. He slid it into a kidney holster beneath his sport coat, then stuffed the spare magazines from the musette bag into his pockets.

"I'll put your gun in your purse," he said to Desiree, as he extracted a .38 S&W Chiefs from the second butterfly rug and loaded it with Nyclads. He dropped the gun and three Safariland speedloaders in the top of her purse on the seat between them. He looked inside the purse as he did. "How you ever going to find your gun in there?" he asked.

"It's a sixth sense women have." She looked at him for a moment and laughed.

He had long ago learned to avoid lengthy conversations with Desiree when she drove—she liked to look at a person as she talked. And that meant not looking at the road.

Track tossed the emptied pistol cases into the musette bag, then the otherwise empty musette bag onto the back seat.

"I feel whole again." He grinned.

"Do you think we'll need the guns?" she asked, glancing at him for an instant.

"Scorese was always a funny guy. I met him twice when I was with CID and once since he left the Company and opened up his executive-protection outfit. All three times I never had the irresistible urge to turn my back on him. Bad vibes or something."

"English is such a bizarre language. Bad vibes—really." And she laughed again.

"We're almost there," Track told her, ignoring the comment.

Desiree was edging the car to the right, taking the ramp and cutting onto Jimmy Carter Boulevard.

TRACK CHECKED HIS WATCH as Desiree turned the white LTD into the office-complex parking lot. Vulcan Executive-Protection Services stood at the far end of the line of brown, single-story buildings, behind lush landscaping.

"Park the car so we don't have to back out," Track told her. "Forget about the signs that say don't back in."

With the car stopped, Desiree put on the emergency brake. "Do me a favor," Track said. "Leave the brake off and move the seat all the way back, then adjust the back a little, too."

"You anticipate we may have to leave in a hurry," she told him, her right eyebrow raising slightly as she looked at him.

"Never hurts to be prepared," Track smiled.

He opened his door and stepped out. It was late fall here, the temperature in the sixties, a moderate breeze blowing from the south. He slammed the door and joined Desiree, standing to one side of the car.

"Hold my purse, Dan."

"Doesn't match my shoes." He smiled, looking at the brown leather bag and then at his black loafers.

He watched her eyes as she slipped her arms into her cream-colored blazer and arranged her hair over the collar of the coat, shaking it free. Taking her bag from him, she hitched it over her shoulder.

They walked along the sidewalk toward the glass door at the far end.

Desiree stopped before the door, and Track reached around her and pulled it open. His eyes caught the gold lettering on the door—Vulcan Executive-Protection Services—and beneath that, in only slightly smaller letters, Peter Scorese, President.

The outer office was carpeted, and at the far end was a solitary desk with an elaborately large call-switching system in one corner, and an electric typewriter on the opposite side. A pretty blonde was working the typewriter.

As Track and Desiree walked toward the desk, there was a dinging sound—a pressure-sensitive panel in the floor, Track guessed—and the receptionist looked up, swiveling her chair toward the center of the desk to face them, smiling. She looked even prettier that way, Track thought—green eyes, blond hair in loose curls, one of them springing down along her forehead. She brushed it away from her eyes. "Hi! Can I help you?"

She wasn't Southern by birth, Track surmised, because the accent was more Midwestern.

"Yes," Track said, smiling back. "My name is Daniel Track, and this is my associate, Miss Goth. I'm an old acquaintance of Peter Scorese and I wanted to consult with him on a matter of extreme importance."

"I'll see if Mr. Scorese is in, sir. If you and Miss

Goth will just make yourselves comfortable," she said as she gestured toward one side where they saw a leather couch, two leather chairs and a glass table topped with more than a dozen current issues of popular magazines. Pedestal ashtrays flanked each end of the couch.

Track and Desiree settled on the couch. As the receptionist began working the switchboard, Track whispered, "Sir Abner checked—Scorese's in town and so he should be here."

In a minute or so, the receptionist leaned forward across her desk, her fingers interlaced beneath her chin as she smiled, "I'm sorry, Mr. Scorese hasn't returned from Stockholm yet. He usually prefers the private entrance and I don't often see him if he is in town. If you have a card you could leave, I'm sure Mr. Scorese or one of his associates will get back to you at the first opportunity."

Track stood. "He isn't in Stockholm—I checked that already. And the Mercedes parked out front is his car—I checked the license plate." Actually, Sir Abner had checked it and Track had merely spotted it by accident as Desiree had parked. "You tell him I want to see him, about the old days when he was in the Company."

"But I'm sorry, sir—as I indicated, his car may be here, but he—"

"I'm sorry, too," Track said, as Desiree rose beside him.

Track started to walk past the desk, Desiree beside him. "Sir! What's—"

"He's going in," Desiree cooed, "and so am I. And you aren't stopping either of us so you might as well make the best impression by just announcing us."

"I'd listen to her, miss, if I were you," Track added, looking at the receptionist as she started out of the chair. "Now, push the door button, miss."

"No—and if you both don't leave I'll call someone to put you out."

"Okay, go ahead," Track responded, and he reached across her desk to the switchboard, punching the com-line button for her. "But don't call the cops. Peter wouldn't like that. Believe me." Track flashed her his biggest smile.

The blonde raised the receiver and spoke into it. "This is Debbie. I need security out here fast. A man and a woman insist on seeing Mr. Scorese."

She hung up and looked at the papers on her desk and began shuffling them.

"Debbie—that's a nice name," Track told her, stepping back a little from the door and tugging Desiree after him. Desiree was reaching into her purse. Track stood with his hands at his sides, his fists tight.

There was an electric buzzing sound, and the door popped open, revealing three men, two in shirt-sleeves, both of these wearing pistols in holsters by their right kidneys. The third man, a sport coat presumably covering his gun, spoke. "You were told that Mr. Scorese is out of town, I understand. Well, he is—"

"You're lying," Track said evenly.

"Look, asshole—" the man began to shout, his voice edgy.

"I'd say I'd beat the crap out of you, but I won't have the chance." Track grinned. The sport-coated man started to say something, but then his eyes widened as he looked at Desiree Goth. The little Chiefs Special was in her right fist, the muzzle less than two inches from his abdomen. The pistol's hammer cocked under her thumb with an audible click. "Now then," Track began. "Have Debbie call Peter Scorese. I want him out here; otherwise, Desiree will shoot you. You don't really need an extra navel—something you can live without, right? And just because it's only a .38 Special, don't figure your hospitalization will bail you out. Those hollowpoints are tipped with a curare derivative in a Teflon-coated sack that'll rupture once the bullet contacts anything even remotely solid. You'll be dead before you can say ouch." That wasn't quite true—they were ordinary Nyclad hollowpoints, no poison-filled sacks of curare to attack the nervous system. But it was the kind of urban-commando thing Track thought the man would fall for. As Track watched the man's eyes, watching his tongue dart from between the too-even teeth to lick his lips, the man turned to Debbie.

She was looking at both of them, her eyes wide. Track couldn't tell if her expression betrayed fear or amusement or a little of both.

"Call Mr. Scorese. Get him out here," the man in the sport coat snapped.

"Yes, Mr. Holland—right away," Debbie answered. Track decided that it was definitely amusement. "Mr. Scorese," Debbie began, clearly taking some delight in the turn of events. "The woman accompanying Mr. Track has a handgun pointed at Mr. Holland, and Mr. Track has indicated the bullets are filled with some kind of poison. Mr. Holland has requested that you join him in the foyer."

Track laughed out loud, watching the girl's eyes widen still more as she drew the phone away from her ear, stared at it and then hung it up quickly.

Track stepped back another pace, glancing behind him to cover both the door leading outside and the inner-office door as he drew the TZ-75, closing his fist around the smooth walnut grip.

Two more men, both wearing suits, both with pistols in their hands filled the office doorway. "Go ahead," Track snapped. "Five of you—two of us. Probably won't kill more than three or four of you before we go down, get the whole office shot to pieces. Put them away or use them—now!" Desiree's body was shielded by the man the receptionist had called Mr. Holland, and Track figured he could empty all fifteen rounds out of the TZ-75 before he went down.

"Put them away like he says," a voice sounded from behind the two men in the doorway. The revolvers disappeared under their jackets as a short man shouldered his way between them.

It was Peter Scorese, his face beaming with a good-natured smile. "Jesus—when Debbie said it was some Mr. Track and some woman, hell, I didn't realize she meant Major Track. Good to see you, Dan!" And Scorese started forward.

"Have them put their guns on Debbie's desk," Track ordered Scorese, stopping him in midstride. The smile faded, then returned almost instantly. Without turning around, Scorese snapped his fingers once. Slowly, each of the five men drew their revolvers, setting them on the desk. "Desiree, pick them up. Anybody moves, Peter has big problems."

Desiree pointed her revolver at Holland's throat as she crossed in front of him, standing beside the desk. She set her bag on Debbie's desk. "Be a dear and hold my purse open for me, Debbie?" One by one, Desiree picked up the five revolvers and placed them in the shoulder bag, then slung it back on her shoulder. "This'll ruin my purse, Dan."

"Sorry, kid," Track told her. He reached under Scorese's jacket and found the butt of a .45 sticking out of a shoulder holster. Track pushed the gun up, then twisted it away from Scorese's body.

"Gee, Dan—why all the gun stuff?" Scorese asked.

"I'm insecure—comes from being orphaned as a youngster, I guess. Where can we talk?"

"My office?"

Track watched Scorese's dark eyes dart left, then right.

"Sure—you first. And remember—" Track slightly shifted the muzzles of the two semiautomatics.

"Hey, we're old comrades in arms. You can put the hardware away. Like I say, if I'd known it was you, hell—"

"Yeah." Track nodded. "Desiree, you take the drag spot behind me."

She turned to the five of Scorese's men. "Because I am a woman, gentlemen, please don't even consider that I might hesitate to kill any or all of you. This revolver has five shots—there are five of you." She gave them a beautiful smile.

Scorese turned toward the doorway and started across the foyer as Track walked after him.

The inner office was carpeted similarly to the foyer, and housed ranks of desks on both sides of a long hall. Small offices had been partitioned off behind the desks. He imagined the offices were for senior staffers, the hallway desks for junior members or people rarely in the office at all. At the moment, the desks and offices were empty. Business couldn't be too good, Track thought. Track pulled

Scorese up before some large double doors at the end of the hallway. "Hold it. I understand you have a Class III license—anybody waiting for us?"

"What—play subguns in my office? You crazy?"

"Yeah, and don't you forget it. Now get inside."

Scorese opened the right-hand door.

Track heard Desiree behind him. "They're still following us," she said.

"Tell your boys to go jerk off in the men's room or something," Track said to Scorese.

"Holland, take the fellas for a walk."

"But, Mr. Scorese—"

"Get their leashes and take them walkies Holland," Track snapped. The tough-guy routine seemed to be working, so he kept it up. "Move it, shithead!"

Track walked inside after Scorese, and Desiree followed them in and closed the door behind them.

"Keep an eye on the door, kid," Track said, handing her the .45.

In his office, Scorese seemed to relax, walking confidently toward his massive walnut desk. Before Scorese could cross to the other side of the desk, Track said, "That's fine, Peter. So, how's things?"

"Just great. How's it going with you, Dan?"

"Couldn't be better, Peter. Hey, listen, the reason we stopped by—"

Scorese's voice dropped. "And I thought you just wanted to play Spillane."

Track smiled. "I was always a great fan of his."

"So, what can I do for you?" Scorese continued.

"Tell me about my sister, Diane, and her husband, Robert Beegh, and the auto accident in 1975."

Track watched Scorese's eyes—they didn't flicker. Self-control, he thought. They should have moved if Scorese hadn't known anything, Track told himself. He pushed it a little harder. "Whose bodies were in the car?"

"I don't know what you're talking about, Dan," Scorese said evenly. "I mean, I knew your sister had died—some buddy of yours told me about it. Sorry. But I don't know what the hell you're talking about. Anyway, what are you digging into something ten years old for?"

"I'm on a nostalgia kick. My sister's alive. And so's my brother-in-law. They're in the Soviet Union." He didn't really expect an answer from Scorese, not a direct one at least.

"I can give you the names of a few guys I know who still work for the Company. Maybe they can help you, Dan. But I don't—"

"My ass—"

"Get the hell out of my office, Track," said Scorese, suddenly getting mean. "And take the—"

"Don't—not a word about her."

"Look, if your brother-in-law and your sister are

still alive—terrific. You should maybe check with State Department about verifying it or—"

"Who died in the car crash? Why was it set up to look like they died?"

"How the hell would I know?"

"Because they're only inside the Soviet Union for one of two reasons. Either it was some kind of game the Company was playing to use Robert and Diane to get information from the Soviets, or it was some kind of game the KGB was playing to use Robert and Diane for their own purposes. Either way, you'd know about it."

"Shit, I can see why you're acting so weird—you're fuckin' crazy, Track."

"Yeah, sure I am. But you go tell whoever it is you should tell that I'm going after Diane and Robert. And I'm going to get them out. So if it's some U.S. operation, they better let me know real quick before I blow it." Track holstered the TZ-75, letting his coat fall over it. "Desiree, give the man his gun. Don't even bother unloading it."

Desiree crossed the room, taking Scorese's Colt from Track's hand and setting it down on the desk.

"Give him his friends' guns, too." Track watched her as she set her bulging purse on the desk and removed the five identical Smith revolvers one at a time. The men outside would have other guns by now, anyway, Track told himself. Desiree made her own revolver disappear inside the bag.

She nodded at Track and smiled. "You try carrying a purse with five loaded guns in it sometime."

Track looked at Scorese. "Get on the phone and tell Debbie you don't want Holland and his playmates messing with us."

"Hey," Scorese said, holding his hands up. "Armed lunatic invades suburban Atlanta security firm—"

"Yeah, I know—details at eleven, right? Wrong. Just ask yourself how many of your clients are insured by one of the member companies of the Consortium. If I don't make it out of the office with Desiree, you're gonna be real unpopular. Fleets of automobiles, industrial parks, office buildings—all with no insurance against all the possible hazards of twentieth-century life."

"Get outta here," Scorese snarled.

"You just remember to tell whoever you've got to tell, Peter."

"When you were in CID, I always thought you were a prick."

"You just remember that, because you were right." Track turned his back and walked toward the double doors with Desiree. He stopped beside the doors, and without turning around said, "Peter—the telephone?"

He heard the sound of the telephone being taken off the cradle. "This is Scorese, Debbie. Put Holland on. Then get him, dammit—yes, now!" There was a long pause that Track filled by clipping the butt end of a Cuesta-Rey Six-T, then lighting the cigar in the blue-yellow flame of his Zippo. "Holland? No, don't do that. Let them both out—don't even look at them cross-eyed. No, he's not pointing a gun at me. Just do it. Then get in here after they're gone—just you."

Track looked at Desiree and their eyes met. He knew that she knew. They would get out of the office—but after that? Scorese was ordering up a hit.

Track looked back over his shoulder at Scorese. "Hey, Peter? Have a nice day, huh?"

There was no one in the corridor, and there was no one in the outer office—not even Debbie—as Track and Desiree started toward the car. He had specifically rented an LTD with the heavy-duty trailer-towing package—a larger radiator, heavy-duty shocks and, most important, the same engine Ford used for police interceptors.

Track slid behind the wheel. Desiree was beside him, buckling herself in as he gunned the engine to life. He put the LTD into overdrive, then set the TZ-75 on the seat beside him under his right thigh. He flicked the safety on—it might be a bumpy ride, he thought.

18

Track held to the speed limit, studying the rearview mirror every few moments. Desiree had twisted around in her seat and was staring out the back window. "I think Mr. Scorese's minions are after us," she announced.

"Minions—that's a good word. I like that," Track said to her, glancing into the rearview. The minions were apparently driving a gray van and coming up fast. "Looks like the minions to me, all right," he told her.

"Don't make fun of me. Zulu taught me how to speak English as well as I do. I grew up speaking French and German, remember?"

"Sometimes I think Zulu swallowed a dictionary. Keep down—I don't think that'll be Holland or any of Scorese's regular employees. Either he had Holland get some local underworld button men with a twenty-four-hour hotline, or it's the KGB."

"They would have had to have followed us, then."

"Yeah, looks that way." He could hear the roar of the van's engine now.

"What about your friend Baslovitch?"

Track looked at her for an instant. His friend Baslovitch—it was an interesting concept, he thought. "If it is the KGB, then Sergei is in deep trouble, I suppose."

"Will he be—" She hesitated.

"Killed? Reprimanded, certainly. Killed, well—they'll try. He's got a reputation as the best man in the Soviet secret service. Respected. Sort of like Allied troops always respected Rommel during World War II. Even though he's the enemy, he's cool, he's the best. I'll tell you one thing—" Track watched the rearview; it was nearly time to see if Sir Abner's remarks about the Ford's engine were based on fact or not "—I wouldn't want to be the guys sent to get Sergei."

"What are you going to do, Dan?"

"About Sergei? Nothing I can do—he knew the chance he was taking."

"About the van?"

"Tighten your seat belt and I'll show you." Track grinned as he looked at her. The van now dominated the rearview mirror.

"I'm buckled up tightly," Desiree said.

"Then hang on." Track stomped the accelerator pedal to the floor. There was a hesitation and then a roar as the LTD threw itself ahead, the power of the engine suddenly unleashed.

Something poked out of the side door of the van—he couldn't be sure if it was a gun—but then the van was gone, the LTD's speedometer over seventy, the van left behind. "Ford does have a better—" Track began.

Gunfire exploded behind them and Track shouted to Desiree, "Down, kid!" as the rear window spiderwebbed.

As the LTD's speedometer needle bounced off the high-speed mark, another blast of gunfire blew out the rear window. Track ducked his head as the car swerved, feeling the impact as the spent slugs imbedded in the seat back. "You all right?" he shouted to Desiree.

"Yes—what are we going to do?"

"This wasn't such a hot plan, right? That's what you're thinking. Go ahead and admit it."

"All right, it wasn't such a hot plan. But what are we going to do now?"

"Panic. That's always good in a situation like this—we'll panic. But meanwhile—" Track cut the wheel hard left as he looked up. In the rearview he could see a subgun coming out of the side door of the van.

The traffic light ahead was against them, and Track cut into the empty oncoming lanes. Track could now see two sets of Mars lights behind the van—police. Taking a left at the corner, he accelerated past a fast-food restaurant and pulled into a cul-de-sac.

"We're trapped!" Desiree screamed at him.

"I *told* you to stay home—now keep down,"

Track snarled, looking into the side-view mirror. The van was taking the corner, and the screech of the tires as they were tortured by the asphalt was suddenly lost as a riot shotgun opened up from the front passenger seat. "Don't worry about the shotgun, he's out of range," Track said as he cut the wheel left, hitting the brakes, aiming for the rear of the cul-de-sac. "Hang on tight, sweetheart," he yelled. Suddenly, Track stomped the LTD's emergency brake, locking the rear wheels and sending the car into a skid as he pulled the wheel all the way to the left. When the rear end was nearly 180° around, he reached down for the brake release, stomping on the gas as hard as he could. Smoke rose in the rearview mirror as the tires dug into the pavement. The wheel spun in his hands as he gave the Ford all the gas he could.

It was a maneuver the van couldn't manage without flipping over, and Track guessed it had bought him twenty seconds—if he could get past the van.

Track held the TZ-75 in his right fist and stabbed the pistol through the open driver's window. Coming up on the blind side of the van he could see the shotgunner raising his gun.

Track's thumb worked the safety up and he double-actioned the first shot into the windshield of the van. The windshield suddenly started to spiderweb.

"Keep down, Desiree!" he yelled.

Track emptied his pistol into the cab and the van swerved out of control. Track threw himself down across the seat, his seat belt released, his left hand locked to the lowest portion of the steering wheel as he brought his foot down hard on the gas pedal.

The roar of a riot shotgun followed, and Track felt the glass as the windshield exploded into a thousand tiny icelike fragments and peppered his body.

Desiree screamed.

"Stay down," he shouted.

When he looked up he saw two police cars blocking the exit from the cul-de-sac.

They were there, and then suddenly one of them was gone, a fireball of black and orange replacing it.

"Holy shit," Track whispered into the wind. Someone had fired a LAW rocket or the equivalent and the police car with however many police officers had been inside it were gone in the snap of a finger.

A second van had pulled up behind the police cars, and as police officers scrambled from their car a figure at the side door of the van shouldered something that looked like a small bazooka.

"Rocket!" Track shouted to Desiree, cutting the wheel hard right, bouncing over the curb.

But it was the second police car that exploded, and another black-and-orange fireball belched upward.

Track brought the big car off the curb and back into the street, part of the left front fender ripping away as the LTD clipped a fireplug. Behind them, the gray van was coming.

"Load my gun!"

"Let's leave the car—we're better off on foot!" Desiree shouted.

"Good thinking." Track cut the wheel hard left, tapping the foot brake, the car skidding, the rear end gliding toward the nearest of the still-burning wrecks of the police cars.

"Run for it—my side," Track commanded, throwing the transmission into park and killing the engine.

He loaded his own gun as he moved through the now open driver's door, Desiree sliding across the seat.

Track let down the slide stop of the TZ-75, leveling it toward the open side door of the white van.

"Shit!" He looked at Desiree. "Run!"

He grabbed her wrist and dragged her from the car.

The air reverberated with a *whoosh* sound, and with his arm encircling her shoulders, Track dived to the road surface, throwing his body over hers.

The ground shook with an explosion, and Track felt a scorching heat slam into the back of his neck and the backs of his hands like a blowtorch.

Track looked back. The LTD was gone.

"Up, kid," he said as he hauled Desiree to her feet and started running toward the wrecked police cars, skirting the burning LTD by a wide margin.

In the van, the man with the LAW rockets was raising another tube to his right shoulder.

Track snapped the TZ-75 on line. "Die, asshole!" he screamed as he pumped the trigger, sending 2-round semiauto bursts hammering toward the rocket man. Desiree was beside him, and he heard the sound of her Model-60 discharging. The rocketeer was stumbling backward.

He heard someone scream, "Jesus—look out!"

Suddenly, the white van was transformed into a tongue of flame licking upward and a fireball bursting literally across the end of the street.

The rocket had discharged inside the van.

Track punched the magazine release for the TZ-75 and rammed a fresh magazine into the butt as he wheeled toward the gray van.

The van had pulled to a halt, and two men were emerging—one was armed with a subgun, the other was poking the air with a riot shotgun.

There was nothing else to do except shoot or die. Track worked the slide release of the TZ-75, touching his index finger to the trigger and fired a 2-shot burst toward the subgunner as the riot shotgun discharged. Track felt the pellets skip off the pavement and sting his shins. Desiree shouted something, but there wasn't time to look.

Track shifted the muzzle from left to right, from shotgunner to subgunner, and fired even bursts of lead. He heard the sound of Desiree's gun barking beside him—but there just wasn't time to look and see if Desiree was wounded.

He only had time to kill.

Finally there was only one shot left in his pistol, and the slide locked open.

If there was a third man in the van, he was dead—there was no time to reload.

Then he heard Desiree's voice. "It's all right, Dan. You killed them—you killed both of them."

Sirens screamed in the distance, and Track dropped into a crouch, staring over his shoulder and the smoldering chunks of metal that had been two police cars, a rented car and a white van.

If the two policemen hadn't run from their vehicle, they would have been dead. He thought of that as he saw one of them approaching cautiously, a service revolver extended in his right hand like a wand to ward off evil, his face ashen, the muzzle of the revolver shaking slightly. The voice not firm at all. "Hold it! Freeze!"

A second policeman appeared, a revolver clutched in both fists. "You heard him—don't even twitch!"

Both of them were very young, Track thought, slowly setting the spent TZ-75 on the pavement. Heat still shimmered from the wrecks in waves, and small popping sounds punctuated the wail of the sirens, all of it carried to him on the hot wind along with the acrid smell of burning gasoline.

"I said, don't move—not a bit!" the younger of the two policemen shouted, not sounding confident at all.

"You bet," Track told the man.

Track looked up at Desiree. "I'm all right," she said, trying to smile. "But you—your pants—they're torn and there's blood and—"

Track breathed a long, loud sigh. "Nothing some Band-aids won't fix, kid." And then he shouted to the two policemen again. "Relax, guys—I'm not moving. Honest!"

Then he started to smile, wondering how Sir Abner would talk them out of this one.

19

Peter Scorese worked his sweating palms along the fronts of his trousers, shifting his feet under the library chair.

And then the door opened.

Her youth always amazed him. They had met three times before. Her hair was dark brown this time, and he liked the color on her. Her usually brilliant eyes were partially hidden beneath a pair of round-framed glasses.

The last time he'd seen her, she'd been dressed like a hooker or someone trying to look like one—he hadn't quite been sure which. But this time, her hair was straight and well past her shoulders, like a wave following after her as her head turned. He wondered if it was hers.

And then doubt beset him—was it really Hummingbird?

He watched her intently.

She wore a blue pleated plaid skirt, like a schoolgirl would wear, a white short-sleeved blouse, and a dark blue sleeveless V-necked sweater.

No, it wasn't Hummingbird, he thought as the woman walked from the doorway and came toward him.

She stopped at the line of bookshelves nearest to him—Biography.

Scorese stared at a magazine, but still he watched her from the corner of his eye.

Finally, she was walking back toward him.

He could hear the sound of her skirt as it brushed over her nylon-stockinged legs.

He wondered what she was like—in bed.

She sat in the chair opposite him. "The library was a poor choice at this time of the day—not crowded enough," Hummingbird whispered.

"I wouldn't meet you where you wanted," he said to her, still glancing at his magazine.

"You were no doubt afraid I would have you killed for your incompetence—but I wouldn't have, Peter."

"I've got to talk to Potempkin."

"But Potempkin has absolutely no need to talk with you," her voice came back, smooth and assured.

He looked up from the magazine and stared into her eyes. They were brown, slightly darker than her hair. He'd remembered them as blue. "What the hell do you really look like?"

"Like the secret fantasy you wouldn't even tell your pillow at midnight," she said, and then she laughed at him.

"I want to talk to Potempkin!" he demanded, hating her smugness.

"Spare yourself the embarrassment of making me emphasize why he doesn't wish to talk to you."

"I couldn't get through to anyone except the emergency number," Scorese said, realizing he was beginning to whine.

"It is our own fault for giving you a team under your command."

"Hey, that was part of the deal—"

"Yes, well, it is no longer, Peter."

Scorese looked into her eyes again—there was a warmth and a prettiness there, and he knew that any display of friendship was a lie. Hummingbird was a courier, the mouthpiece for Potempkin, the head of station for the KGB in the United States. "So what does he have planned?"

Scorese still looked at her eyes, which smiled as she answered. "Your welfare. You have served us well in the past, and will serve us well in the future." Scorese involuntarily breathed a sigh of relief. "There is no possible way this Major Track can connect you to the two vans and the murders of the policemen. He has already tried. His contact with the insurance cartel, the Englishman Sir Abner Chesterton, has tried. Desiree Goth will likely try, but there is nothing to fear. You acted out of ego." She moved her eyes away from his, appearing to read the contents of the notebook folded open on her lap. "Potempkin does not act out of ego. You dispatched the two teams of men because Track affronted you by making fools of your security people, by taking over your office. You did not send the teams after him because it was the prudent move that would prohibit him from discovering the nature of our facility where Robert Beegh is currently engaged."

"But—"

"Let me finish. All you have done is exactly what Major Track wanted you to do. Somehow—Potempkin is making arrangements concerning this even as we speak—Major Track had reason to believe his sister was still alive. He needed confirmation—that is why he behaved with you as he did. And you did exactly as he desired. He now knows. He is even now preparing to leave Atlanta."

"I can stop that."

"You will not," she scolded him. "Major Track will likely go to India—that information will be confirmed soon—and from India to Pakistan with the hope of penetrating our borders through Afghanistan. But he will not leave India alive. The woman may also die, and if it can be arranged successfully, their deaths will be attributed to her dubious associates in the international arms trade. That is the precise manner in which this little fiasco you engineered will likely be written off—some disgruntled buyer taking his revenge against Desiree Goth and Major Track just getting in the way."

"What the hell is Track's brother-in-law doing over there?"

"That is none of your concern. You are supposedly away on business. I advise you go away after performing one minor task for us. Return in two weeks or so. There will be a few routine questions from the local police and the FBI. Perhaps even some of your old associates in the CIA will come by. Wouldn't that be charming for you, though? I will contact you when we next need your services.

"I will leave my steno pad on the seat after I leave—there is an envelope containing ten thousand dollars inside it. Consider it vacation money—certainly not a bonus for efficiency. There are also the instructions for your assignment. After I am gone, you will discover the notebook as you get ready to leave. Slip the envelope from inside it and take the steno book up to the charge desk and turn it in to lost and found and then leave."

He looked up from his magazine, into her eyes. "What about you?"

She closed her notebook, then hugged it against her chest as a schoolgirl would. "I have homework to do, Mr. Scorese."

20

"We have received this communiqué through Hummingbird from Potempkin, Comrade Commissar Ghermahnyevitch," Colonel Yehrevhenskiy said after clearing his throat.

Ghermahnyevitch looked up. He was slightly amused. "Read it to me."

"Yes, Comrade Ghermahnyevitch." Yehrevhenskiy cleared his throat again. "'Personnel note—recommend code-name-designation change of Agent Sapphire to Agent Albatross, as per "The Rime of the Ancient Mariner."'" Yehrevhenskiy looked up.

"An English poem. The Ancient Mariner had to hang an albatross around his neck—never mind. Go on."

"Continuing then, 'Recommend cleanup from your end per leak. Steps being taken to remove previous subject of Albatross's mistake. Should not reach you.'"

"And?"

"That is all, Comrade. I can verify with the signals foreman—"

"No, it appears Potempkin feels confident this man Track will be eliminated. A pity—a very brave man. But if Potempkin directed Hummingbird to send such a message, there is no doubt in my mind that what needs to be accomplished will be accomplished. Robert Beegh's work cannot be interrupted. In the event Potempkin's plans are unsuccessful, order that security around the installation be heightened. Order that border security near the installation be heightened, as well. Robert Beegh's research is at the breakthrough stage, I have been given to understand. It cannot be interrupted lest a significant strategic advantage be lost or delayed."

"This leak that is spoken of, Comrade?"

Commissar Ghermahnyevitch stood. It was difficult because his legs were stiff from sitting too long already. He walked from behind his desk toward the heavily draped windows looking out onto the square. He opened the draperies, stood resolutely in the window and looked down on the children's park. No one skated—the hour was too late. "I skated when I was a little boy. I enjoyed it very much. But now—" He dismissed the thought. "The leak is Sergei Baslovitch."

"That cannot be, Comrade," Yehrevhenskiy sputtered. "He is—"

"A hero of the Soviet Union many times over—yes, I know. But it is he. He used the computer room prior to departing for Switzerland. Major

Track was in Switzerland at the same time. I believe some sort of bond was struck between the men during the incident at Academgorodok. It is the only logical assumption—Baslovitch acted out of personal motives, perhaps to repay a debt of honor." He stared at the barren skating rink in the park below. "Isn't it curious that we must punish men for friendship, for honor? There can be no trial—he has too many influential friends. Too many of the people know of his heroics. He has become popular. His co-workers look up to him. He delivered the commencement address at the Chicago Espionage School last year. He must be eliminated in such a manner that it appears he has fallen victim to some Western plot. Perhaps it can be made to look as though the British Secret Service or the CIA was responsible directly. I will leave the details to your imagination. But it must be well-done—too many members of the Politburo value Sergei. As I do—so it must be quick."

He let the draperies fall closed. "See to it—that is my order."

Yehrevhenskiy just stared for a moment, then in a voice lifeless as Baslovitch's body would soon be, Yehrevhenskiy murmured, "Yes, Comrade."

Ghermahnyevitch reopened the drapes and he tried to recall his childhood. But he could not recall those days no matter how long he stood there and stared at the ice rink, no matter how long.

21

The movement of Svetlana beside him had awakened him—either that or the gray Moscow sunrise. He was not certain which, but he stared at the ceiling now, wide awake, unable to sleep.

He sat up, lighting a Players—a friend who had just returned from England had brought them to him. He had other ways of getting them, but it was the thought that counted.

He lit one, his first cigarette of the day, inhaling deeply. He glanced at his watch. It was almost seven-thirty.

Sergei Baslovitch looked past the wristwatch, to the still-sleeping Svetlana. She was very beautiful, as dark haired as Tatiana had been fair. He felt himself smile. "Tatiana," he murmured.

Svetlana—a girl in whose bed he had slept often—had been the first for him since the night with Tatiana. And somehow it had been different than the way it had been with Svetlana before Tatiana.

It was not as good.

He stubbed out the cigarette and swung his legs

from under the sheet and over the side of the bed, until his feet rested on the cold wooden floor. He stood up, stretching, his eyes catching sight of the shoulder holster with the P-7 in it suspended from the dressing-table chair. Making love to Tatiana had either been the best experience of his life or the most damaging. He could not tell which, and perhaps it was both. . . .

SERGEI BASLOVITCH had left his car parked near Svetlana's—it was only a two-block walk to his own apartment, and he was counting on the fresh cool air and the exercise to clear his head. But as he stopped in front of the entrance to his apartment building, his brain still felt fogged in.

He wanted to call Tatiana. She would be safely home in Academgorodok by now. But the information she had given him and what he had discovered on his own then and passed to Dan Track might lead to undesired fallout. He would wait. He had no desire to involve the girl in a potentially deadly situation.

Baslovitch shrugged, and began searching the pockets of his gray tweed overcoat for his keys.

He thrust the key into the lock, turned it and worked the knob, passing through the glass-paneled door and into the lobby. A second key was needed—it was a secure building—and he used this to enter the interior hall.

His apartment building depressed him. His

apartment, on the other hand, was a place he truly liked. The building was drab, gray, modern. The apartment contained the small treasures he had acquired in nearly eighteen years of traveling the world in defense of the Soviet people. A *bolo* from Argentina, a large Eye of God wall hanging from the western United States. Venetian glass from the early nineteenth century. But the apartment did not contain the object most on his mind since the short assignment in Germany.

He worked the elevator controls, signaling his floor, and leaned against the wall of the elevator, feeling the motion through the muscles in his back. Yesterday, the doctor had told him the sunglasses would no longer be needed except in the strongest of light. His eyes were nearly healed.

He was grateful for that—the prospect of being blind had frightened him.

The elevator doors opened and he stepped out, turning left. His apartment was at the far end of the corridor and fronted the street.

Something made him pause—something in the ambience of the place, something he could not define. He shook his head, trying to free himself of the feeling as he stood halfway in the middle of the hallway—but the feeling would not leave him. Was it just too many years in the field, he wondered, as a shiver ran down his spine. Or were his senses telling him that now was not the time to forget his training.

He stood there.

He searched his key ring—nothing that would handily get him into the vacant apartment next door to his own.

He reached under his sport coat for the P-7. The chamber was loaded. He held the gun loosely in his right fist, the keys in his left hand as he walked the remaining distance to his front door. The apartment had only one other door, heading to the fire escape. He jabbed the gun into his belt, found his lighter and by the light of the flame looked for telltale scratch marks on his lock.

There was one scratch mark, but he might have made it himself, coming home some night with too much liquor in him. Baslovitch couldn't remember the scratch being there, but couldn't remember its absence clearly, either.

He took the P-7 into his hand again, turning the key in the lock with his left hand.

He let the door swing inward, but didn't walk inside. He held the P-7 loosely, so the noise of the squeeze cocker wouldn't betray on which side of the doorframe he stood.

There was no sound.

"Getting old," he told himself, laughing at himself. He approached the doorway with caution, anyway.

With his left hand, Baslovitch tossed the half-empty package of Players through the door. Nothing happened.

He shrugged and started through the doorway. Then he heard the voice behind him.

"Drop your gun, Sergei. Please do not make us kill you yet."

Inside his apartment he could see three men, two of whom he recognized immediately, the third looked vaguely familiar.

And the voice from behind him? The vacant apartment, of course. The door lock had probably been taped and the hinges oiled so there would be no noise when the door was opened. Perhaps some smell of the oil had originally alerted him. It was too late to care.

"What if I do not drop my gun? If you plan to kill me anyway, what purpose would it serve?"

There was no immediate answer. The three men inside wore gloves and carried silenced MAC-10 submachine guns. For some reason, the KGB wanted it to appear as though the CIA had caused his death, Baslovitch thought, looking at the guns. "You were not told to do it this way," Baslovitch said suddenly, still standing in his doorway.

"I could not do it the way it was ordered, not without telling you that it is not a personal thing, Sergei. Why they wish you dead I have not been told. I only made certain it was not some sort of mistake." Baslovitch recognized the voice of the man behind him—Ivan Petrovitch. They had lunched together yesterday. "But I did not wish for you to die thinking a friend had betrayed you. I do only what I am ordered to do."

"I appreciate that more than I can say, Ivan. A last cigarette? You can hardly say it will be damaging to my health."

"What about the gun?"

"I'll keep the gun—but no tricks while I light the cigarette."

Petrovitch's voice from behind him: "Mikhail, give Comrade Major Baslovitch his package of cigarettes."

As one of the three subgunners started forward to pick up the package of Players, Baslovitch said, "And before I die, I have enjoyed the cigarettes very much, Ivan—thank you."

"You are welcome, my old friend."

"I'm putting away my keys and taking out my lighter. That means shifting the gun to my left hand."

"That is acceptable, Sergei."

"Thank you." Baslovitch pocketed the keys, shifted the gun to his left hand and searched his pockets for the lighter. Mikhail extended a cigarette to Baslovitch and Baslovitch took it between his lips, lit it and pocketed his lighter. He didn't bother to shift the gun back to his right hand. Without turning around, he asked Ivan, "They told you nothing?"

"Only that it was for the good of the state and involved highly secret work. That is all. Why do they wish this thing done?"

Baslovitch shrugged. "You know how they are—paranoid bastards. But I'm sure they endured a great deal of soul searching before ordering my execution. You are just going to shoot me?"

"Yes, and leave one of the American submachine guns. Does that strike you as plausible?"

"I am to be the heroic victim of United States imperialism?"

"Yes, I think so, Sergei." And then Petrovitch laughed. "Perhaps they will build a statue to you at the Chicago school."

Baslovitch shrugged, but slowly so none of them would think he was going for a gun—yet. "You realize," he said, and exhaled a cloud of gray cigarette smoke. The cigarette had almost burned down, and for the first time in his life he wished that he smoked cigars. "You realize," Baslovitch said again, "that I won't just let you kill me, Ivan. And please, there is nothing personal to it."

"I would prefer that you would have a chance. Each of us is prepared to die if necessary."

"No one is prepared to die—that's a silly idea. But not yet—I'm still smoking. It will look better if there are bloodstains and the signs of a fight."

"I agree completely, Sergei."

"Well, then we had better be about it," Baslovitch continued. He snapped his cigarette into Mikhail's face, pumping the trigger of the P-7 twice, putting a slug into each of the remaining two men in front of him as he threw his body across the room and through a doorway. Submachine-gun fire filled the air as he rolled onto his back and fired into Mikhail, the man's submachine gun turning toward him. Mikhail's neck pumped blood as Baslovitch reached up, shooting Mikhail's right hand to loosen the death grip on the MAC, Mikhail's body rocking with hits as Petrovitch and one of the wounded men opened fire.

Baslovitch had the MAC, and he directed it like a hose toward the two wounded men. Suddenly his left hand erupted in pain and blood. He threw himself behind the sofa, and even as machine-gun fire shredded the upholstery, he was running, diving through the open bedroom door.

"Sergei! Do not—"

He didn't hear the rest. He scooped up a copy of *War and Peace* and threw it through the bedroom window leading to the small balcony that in turn led to the fire escape. The glass shattered outward, but instead of taking the escape route he skidded into the bathroom and shut the door.

Throwing the lid of the flush tank to the floor, he reached inside and hauled out a plastic bag. The water in the tank was red with clouds of blood from his wounded hand.

He ripped open the bag and took out a stun grenade. As the bathroom door slivered under the impact of subgun slugs, he pulled the pin.

Baslovitch ripped back the shower curtain and

threw himself into the bathtub, looking for protection of any kind.

Pinging sounds creased the air as slugs hit the toilet and the tub. Then the gunfire stopped.

For a few seconds, nothing happened. Then the door was kicked open, and Baslovitch flipped the grenade toward the door and buried his head in his hands, covering his ears against the sound, squinting his eyes shut against the light.

He counted until the sound and the light would have died.

Then he was on his feet, the MAC in both fists, spraying through the doorway. Stepping out of the tub, he moved past the bullet-smashed toilet and into the bedroom. He emptied the MAC, and Petrovitch screamed as a 3-round burst slammed through his skull.

He found the other man behind the bed. A bullet had gone through his eye and taken away the back of his head as it exited.

Baslovitch checked the front room, but nobody rose to greet him. Petrovitch had only brought the three men, but no doubt more would soon be on the way. Firefights had a way of drawing attention.

He walked back into the bedroom, set down the MAC and starting to grab the few things that he could carry and would need—the P-38 he had brought home from the office, the five 50-round boxes of 9mm ammo, the spare magazines for the

P-7. He took the pistol from his belt and set it on the dresser.

What he had feared might happen, had happened.

Russia would no longer be his home.

He would miss Petrovitch and the others like him—friends of long standing.

Escape routes out of the country would be blocked—he would be looked for, Baslovitch knew.

In his mind, a plan already was forming. Dan Track would somehow find a way to penetrate the Soviet Union, to reach the base where Robert Beegh did his work, where Track's sister Diane would be.

And Track would have an escape route—Desiree Goth would see to that for him.

He would go there and wait for Track, use Track's escape route—it was the only solution.

Grabbing an old T-shirt, Baslovitch wound it tightly around his bloodied hand and made for the door.

22

"I really don't like to talk about it."

"It must have been just terrible, George—your uncle and you both getting shot."

"He was fine—just a flesh wound."

"The operations—I remember how strong you were. When I'd come into your room at the hospital, never once did you—"

George looked up into her green eyes. "Are you glad you took your vacation here with me?"

She didn't answer for a moment. "Well, I just thought that maybe you needed a nurse around after all the pain you had endured. So I came."

"But is that the only reason you came?"

She leaned over and kissed the tip of his nose. "You know it isn't, George."

He reached up, knotting his fingers into her dark hair, pulling her head down toward him, kissing her lips—they were moist, warm. She tasted good to him.

"Would you like a sandwich or something?" she said, slipping her lap from under his head, sliding off the couch.

George's head bounced against the seat cushion and he turned his head to follow her with his eyes, but Dorothy the wonder cat was on the table beside the couch and she stretched and rubbed her nose against his. "Get outta here," he snarled good-naturedly. "What's with females and my nose all of a sudden?" Then he stood slowly, because his abdomen was still tender from the last operation and probably from the one before that, too. But he got to his feet and started across the living room and toward the kitchen after Kate. Dorothy ran beside him, outdistancing him as he walked, taking a flying leap, settling on the kitchen counter. Kate turned away from the refrigerator and walked over to the counter, stroking Dorothy's head and neck.

"Who was that really pretty older woman you introduced me to—I forgot her name," Kate asked as George settled onto a stool beside the counter.

"That was Tassels LaTour, my uncle's secretary."

"And she comes up here every day—" Kate broke into baby talk, still patting Dorothy, now staring Dorothy right in the eye "—just to feed little you, isn't that right, kitten?" Then Kate looked away from the cat and into George's eyes. "That nice Miss. . . LaTour?"

"LaTour, yeah."

"She said if I want while I'm here I can drive

down into Albuquerque and join one of her dance classes. She told me she appeared all over the United States and Europe when she was younger. She has a dancer's legs—you can tell that."

"That's not all she's got," George told her.

"She said it was Middle Eastern dancing and acrobatic dancing and tap—"

"She was one of the most famous strippers in the world."

Kate's eyes widened. "George! That's not a nice thing to say about the woman. Especially after you were so nice to her."

George lit a cigarette with a disposable lighter. "What do you mean, she told you I was so nice to her?"

"Taking her out to dinner that time. She told me she had a lovely time with you." Kate walked around the counter and wrapped her arms around George's neck. "It's so nice to find a man like you. You're so sweet, George." She kissed him hard on the mouth. George discovered a special portion of his anatomy was still gifted with finely honed reflexes.

"Why don't we skip the sandwiches? We can go into—"

"Remember what the doctor said, George? You might hurt your incision."

"I'm almost healed. Look, I'll show you."

"I washed you in the hospital every day—I know

you're almost healed. But we have to give it a little more time."

"I don't want to give it any more time, Kate, for—"

She kissed him again. "In another few days." She ducked around the counter before he could stop her.

He sat on the stool, staring at her as she made headcheese sandwiches. He didn't like headcheese, and wondered what form of life did.

The telephone rang.

"I'll get it—you just sit still," Kate commanded.

George nodded, staring at the sandwiches. Dorothy sat on the other end of the counter, and he muttered to Dorothy under his breath, "Eat my sandwich, Dorothy—eat my sandwich dammit. You go after everything else—eat the sandwich."

"George—it's for you," Kate called.

George stood up from the stool and started around the counter and toward the telephone on the far wall by the back door.

He took the telephone from Kate, and she slipped away back toward the counter. "This is George Beegh."

The voice on the other end of the line was totally unfamiliar. "This is a friend of your uncle's—only I think your uncle is doin' you dirt."

"Fuck off!" George snapped into the phone. He saw Kate turn around from the counter to look at him.

The voice on the other end of the line went on. "Your mother and father died in 1975 in an auto accident—only it wasn't an accident and they didn't die, and Dan Track knows it, but he's not tellin' you. Check with Sir Abner Chesterton if you don't believe me."

And the line clicked dead.

"George, I'm surprised at you," Kate said, her tone light and playful. "Such language. I know you've been ill, but I would never have thought—"

But George was already dialing Sir Abner's 800 number in New York City.

"Now, you apologize to me for talking that way or I'll. . ." Kate went on.

Without looking at her, George snapped, "What—feed me some more goddammed head-cheese sandwiches! Just shut up!"

It was a very long call, and it didn't help that Kate was standing in the living room staring out the window, her arms folded in front of her, and that his abdomen was really starting to hurt from standing for such a long time. Finally, he told Sir Abner Chesterton, "Dan has no damn right to hold back on me."

"That was probably Scorese on the telephone, George. Dan is on his way to try and verify the data even as we speak, and if Scorese is working for the opposition, then Scorese would want you going in there after Dan just to complicate things."

"Look, I took care of myself all those years in

the Air Force and I can take care of myself now. If Dan can get into the Soviet Union to search for my mother and father, dammit, so can I—with or without your help!"

"But—"

"Are you going to help or do I—"

"You can't just barge into Soviet territory as if you were going on some overseas holiday," Chesterton persisted.

"What's it going to be, Sir Abner?"

"But I can't even reach Dan."

"What's it going to be?"

"Yes, yes, just as you bloody well knew it would be. But—"

"I'll see you in New York." George slammed down the receiver.

He looked around and saw Kate standing by the kitchen door. "I didn't know..." she began.

"That I don't like headcheese?"

"No—but that, too, I guess."

"I'm sorry I yelled at you."

"Is it really true—you're going into Russia?"

"It's more Asia, really—a city called Alma Ata. And yeah, I'm going there."

"You might not come back."

"I'm going there, anyway."

He was beside her now, and she stared up at him. "Then come to bed with me first," she said.

George glanced at his watch. It was five hours

until the next direct flight to New York. And she was an awfully pretty girl.

George walked toward her and took her in his arms. "Why? Because maybe I won't come back?"

"No. Because I like you—even if you're a shit and you don't like headcheese."

But he liked honesty in a woman, and he kissed her hard on the mouth.

23

Dan Track sat beyond the open balcony doors, the breeze ruffling in his hair. He realized he was feeling calmer than he had any right to feel. He watched the reflection of the sun on the Yamuna river, the water shimmering in long splashes of gold. The fireball had considerable distance to go before it slipped below the horizon, and he was alternately saddened and gladdened by the fact. Nightfall would mean sleeping with Desiree and being with her in the fullest sense words could imply. Nightfall would then lead to dawn, and at dawn he would slip away from the hotel and meet the contact Desiree had arranged who would fly him across the border into Pakistan.

He decided to occupy his mind with something else. He and Desiree had spent that afternoon walking through the narrow and winding streets of Delhi, a city that had its roots in the twelfth century and had once been part of the Mogul empire. Along Chandni Chawk he had bought a silver ornament for her hair.

The whine of the hair dryer alerted him that Desiree was out of the shower.

He continued to stare down into the teeming city and along the river, trying to see the point where the Yamuna and the Ganges joined. It was a holy spot to the Hindus, and a holy spot might well be a good thing to see.

Once they were in Pakistan, Desiree's smuggling contacts would help him get into Afghanistan. And then he had the trek across the strife-torn mountains toward Alma Ata. There would be answers there. Beyond the Hindu Kush.

Track stood up from the balcony edge, turning away from the sun and the Yamuna river and the throbbing city that surrounded him and walked across the sitting room of their suite to the small table beside the couch.

He picked up the Walther P-5 that one of Desiree's contacts had provided for him, mechanically removing the magazine, checking for a loaded chamber, reinserting the magazine. It might be very nice, he thought, to go for a walk with his girl without needing to worry that someone might try to kill them.

He noticed now that the noise of the hair dryer had stopped, how long ago he didn't know.

Hearing the sounds of movement, he looked up to see Desiree walking toward him. She wore a full-skirted dress of silk, the color like that of rich cream stirred into coffee, the dress nearly touching the floor. Wound about her was a traditional sari, the rich gold fabric interwoven with threads of silver. A portion of the sari was drawn up over her head to cover her hair, not veiling her face but rather accenting it. The silver ornament hung from her hair and across her forehead, stopping just short of her eyebrows, her eyes cast downward. "You're lovely," he told Desiree.

She raised her eyes, their blueness absorbing him. "When in Rome—"

"Dress as the Romans?"

"Yes, something like that."

"I'm very pleased we're not somewhere where people bundle themselves in layers of furs, then."

"I love you very much," she whispered.

"I already knew that," he told her.

"Shall we go for our walk?"

He looked at the gun in his hand for a moment, then looked around the room for his jacket as he shoved the gun into the waistband of the trousers of his tan suit. "Just the three of us," he said to her....

THE SKY to the west was a wash of purple and the muezzins called the faithful as Dan Track held Desiree Goth's hand and walked with her through the streets of Delhi.

All eyes focused on her, some boldly, some furtively. He liked being alone with her, but almost equally he liked being with her in public. In the four years they had known each other, he had never ceased to appreciate the looks of envy that she was his. He said to her, "You've been in India before, haven't you?"

"With the brisk business of late in Afghanistan, it's a convenient place to consummate a deal."

"Make sure that's all you consummate if I'm not around," Track said, laughing.

"Do you consider that I belong to you?"

She stopped walking and Track turned and looked into her eyes. "Yes," he said.

Desiree smiled. "That's good—because I feel that way, too." And they began to walk again.

The muezzins' calls went on. Some of those in the winding street seemed resolutely to ignore the call, while others moved quickly. Some were Hindu, some Moslem, and it was the Moslems being called to their sunset prayers.

Track and Desiree walked toward the principal mosque in Delhi, the Jāmi' Masjid. It was one of the many mosques from the old Sultanate of Delhi, commissioned by the conquering Moslems, crafted by the subjugated Hindus and reflecting the culture and the design of both religions.

Backwashed with the purple of the sky and wisps of white cloud along the artificial horizon beyond, the chocolate-drop-shaped archways formed the eastern wall of the roofless structure that surrounded the mosque within. Behind the arcade lay an ornamental garden. A central, massive arch, perhaps fifty feet high, formed the main entranceway.

Desiree began to speak beside him as they walked down the low steps leading to the square the mosque dominated. "I'll confess it wasn't merely romanticism on my part that was behind our taking a walk precisely now and precisely here."

"I was afraid you were going to say that."

"There is a man we must meet—to confirm that all is well for tomorrow. His name is Benjamin Faring-Brown. It sounds English, but he is more than half Hindu. A young man—very smart, very clever."

"How long will Mr. Faring-Brown tie us up?"

"Only a few minutes. Then we can watch the sunset until it is finished. You can order supper up to our suite if you like."

Men were spreading prayer rugs beyond the eastern wall now, and Track and Desiree stopped a respectful distance from the wall. Track could put himself in the position of the worshippers—trying to pray and being forced to stare at a man and a woman who did not share the same faith.

"Let's wait here."

Desiree stood close beside him, and he felt the softness of her flesh against his hands, the smoothness of the silk of her sari. The purpling sky darkened her eyes. He thought about what awaited him at Alma Ata. If the KGB was behind his sister's disappearance, something made him feel that her husband was somehow behind it, too. And if Robert was involved in some incredible evil for the Russians, Track wondered about killing the man, his brother-in-law. Would he hesitate to kill Robert Beegh because almost all his life he had wanted to throttle the man? Would he kill Robert too quickly, too hastily because of this?

How would he tell George? "Son, look, I had to kill your dad."

If he survived, Dan Track thought, he'd deal with it.

"Miss Desiree?"

The voice drew him back—very clipped, an odd mixture of British and stage East Indian.

Track looked to the sound of the voice. "Dan," Desiree's voice began from beside him, "this is the young man I mentioned, Benjamin Faring-Brown."

Track extended his right hand. Benjamin Faring-Brown was a full head shorter than him and slightly built, almost appearing molded into a white tropical suit, a white shirt and a blue polka-dot bow tie. The slicked-back black hair was gleaming in the dying sun and the dark eyes smiled. "Miss Desiree has spoken about you very much, Major Track. I am very pleased to meet you after all this time."

The handclasp was firm, dry.

"And I'm pleased to meet you. What do your friends call you?"

"Benny, actually, Major."

"Dan'll do fine."

"Quite. Dan it shall be." His eyes flickered toward Desiree.

Track laughed. "I can't take my eyes off her, either. What have you got for us, Benny?"

"Yes—Benny." Desiree laughed.

"She calls me Benjamin, but she is the only one," Faring-Brown explained to Track. "I have a slight change in plans. We will still leave at seven in the morning, but the pilot became ill. But if Major Track can fly us in, I can engage a pilot in Pakistan to fly me back here."

"No problem. What kind of plane?"

"A propeller-driven craft, Major."

"How many propellers?"

"Two."

"Two—I just don't like odd numbers over three, that's all. We're all set, Benny."

"All the requirements you indicated, Miss Desiree," he went on, "have been fulfilled. The appropriate weapons and climbing gear are packed and ready."

"You've done well, Benjamin," Desiree said as Track looked at her. "That's why I count on you so much here. I'd invite you to share supper with us, Benjamin, but it will be Major Track's and my last evening together until his return. You understand, of course."

"Of course, Miss Desiree. I shall wait for Major Track outside the hotel at six-thirty tomorrow morning."

"Wonderful, Benjamin," Desiree told him.

"Until tomorrow then, Major?"

Track shook Faring-Brown's hand again.

Desiree extended her hand, Faring-Brown taking it. "If I may be permitted." He bent over Desiree's hand and touched his lips to it, then turned and walked into the crowd.

Track watched after Faring-Brown a moment, then turned to Desiree, mimicking Faring-Brown and Zulu. "Miss Desiree, how many men would die at your whim?"

"I haven't counted lately, but I imagine the number is rather large by now."

Track folded his arms around her, staring back toward the mosque.

In the arch nearest to the center and to his right Track saw something. "An evening star—I just—" But in the instant, Track realized that it wasn't a star but a reflection, perhaps from some light source behind him...perhaps. Someone beside him screamed, and Track pushed Desiree toward the wall butting the steps leading down from the street above. Looking behind him he saw a turbaned man crumpling across the rough stone steps, his gray shirt splotched red with blood at the breastbone. As the man fell forward, Track caught a glimpse of the exit wound before the body rolled away—the size of a half grapefruit and torn at the edges. But there had been no sound.

Track's hand snaked under his suitcoat, finding the butt of the Walther stuffed in his trouser band. As he jabbed the pistol toward the small arch, a chunk of stone near Desiree's face tore away, and Desiree sucked in her breath loudly, drawing back, covering her face with the cloth of the sari, pressing her body close against him.

"Stay behind me," Track commanded, gripping the Walther P-5 in both hands. Screams and shouted epithets erupted from the crowd as panic swept like a brushfire across the square. Rock powdered in a fine cloud inches from his head, and Track steadied the Walther against the rock wall and thumbed back the hammer for single action, tripping the trigger as he settled the sights on the portion of the arch where he had seen the reflection of the sniper scope.

He held high. The range, shooting at an upward angle—all of it mitigated against him.

The trigger broke under finger pressure. The pistol rocked imperceptibly in his fists.

Suddenly a figure was silhouetted in the archway.

Profiled against the purple sky, it tumbled from the arcade and to the ground. Shouts rose from the base of the wall as men ran toward the steps, knives brandished high over their heads, anger a mask for their faces. A police siren sounded on the edge of the square.

Track glanced at Desiree. "That was a miraculous shot," she said.

"Hey, what can I say. I shoot like that all the time," he lied, but knowing that she knew he was lying made it all right. "Run with me—now!"

And Track worked the P-5's decocking lever as he shoved the gun into his waistband and shouldered his way into the crowd. People screamed at him, and Desiree shouted from beside him, "They are calling you a murderer."

"Great. Flattery—I love it."

A man thrust a knife from the crowd and Track dodged back, shielding Desiree's body with his own. He didn't know who was a civic-minded citizen filled with righteous indignation and who might be working with the now dead sniper.

Track's right arm moved in an outward circle, pushing away the knife hand at the forearm, and he planted his left foot in the crotch of the knife artist, the man's body doubling forward, crumpling at the knees. "Sorry, pal," Track rasped, starting ahead again.

Another man aimed a pistol toward Desiree's face. Track shoved her away as a woman in the crowd shrieked in terror. The pistol discharged, Track falling left, just ahead of the shot, his left shoulder impacting the cobblestones of the steps, his right hand finding the P-5. He double-actioned the trigger, and the assailant's body doubled forward, rolling onto the steps, both hands clasped to the chest.

He was up, finding Desiree, punching a man in

the face who reached for her, grabbing her, half dragging her with him.

He heard his name shouted. "Track!"

Track wheeled toward the sound and saw two men, one Hindu, the other European, the European holding a gun. Track shot him dead where he stood, emptying the P-5 into the man's chest.

The one with the knife lunged forward, and Track backstepped, losing his footing on the steps. The knife man threw himself down. Track's ight hand caught the man's wrist, and his left fist hammered the man's kidney. But the knife wielder's left hand closed tightly on Track's windpipe.

Track punched upward with his left knee, but he was contacting bone, not groin. It was getting harder to breathe and harder to hold the knife back from his chest.

The hand on his windpipe seemed stronger than a vise.

Suddenly the sari interwoven with the silver thread was wound around the knifewielder's neck and his head jerked back, his left hand going to his throat. Track caught the knife hand in both of his hands and rolled with it, outward, away from the body of the knife wielder, slamming the wrist against the edge of one of the cobblestone treads. The bastard shrieked with pain.

Track's right knee smashed upward now, again

and again, and the man's fetid breath assailed Track's nostrils.

The man was to his knees. Track saw Desiree, the sari knotted in her hands, her body twisting away from the knife wielder, his head snapping back. Track, on one knee, crossed the man's jaw with his left, the head craning fast.

Track's eyes found the knife, Track grasping it in his right fist, ramming it into the chest below the sternum.

"I have your gun," Desiree shouted.

"Keep it. It's empty and I did a dumb thing—no spare magazines. Run for it." He was up and moving. Desiree was slightly ahead of him at the top of the steps, the sari bunched in her left hand.

He jumped the last three steps. The police sirens were louder now.

"Here, you keep the gun. I can't hold everything!" Desiree shouted.

He took the P-5 as she jammed it into his hands.

Then a voice came out of the crowd, and Track twisted the pistol in his hands to use the butt like a bludgeon. "Major! Miss! This way!"

It was Benjamin Faring-Brown. He could have fingered them to the sniper, Track realized.

But if Desiree trusted him so much....

Track grabbed Desiree's hand. "Come on, the man's offering us a way out, kid!"

Benjamin Faring-Brown ducked through a small doorway muttering, "This way—hurry!"

Track pushed ahead of Desiree in case it was a trap. He passed through the doorway and heard Faring-Brown's continued entreaty to hurry.

"Into the back!" Faring-Brown urged.

The store was dimly lit, but Track saw another doorway leading into a greater darkness. Desiree shoved past him, racing inside, and Track followed her through.

He heard the sound of a door slamming behind him. Then in the darkness a match was struck. Track still held the empty gun, the butt like a hammer in his right hand.

He followed the movement of the match, and suddenly there was light—a lantern, the glass scratching against the metal of the frame as it was lowered in place. "The store is locked and unoccupied. The police will look at the electric meter perhaps. This way," he said, indicating the lantern, "there is nothing. Follow me, please." Faring-Brown walked past them, toward the rear of the room.

Benjamin Faring-Brown pulled up, saying, "I could well imagine, Major, that you might assume I had pointed out your presence to the sniper, but I did not." In the dim light cast by the lantern, Track could see a Walther P-5 in Faring-Brown's right hand.

"I store many of these pistols here for Miss Desiree's needs. There are spare magazines in this box." Benny set down the pistol beside a wooden crate, opening the lid. Inside were dozens of spare magazines, three identical P-5s and a dozen boxes of American-made 9mm hollowpoints.

Track looked into Desiree's face in the lamplight. "You buy these things by the gross, or what?"

"Well—" she smiled "—I don't exactly buy them, Dan."

"Right." Track nodded, and he started to gather spare magazines for the P-5 in his hand.

24

Track and Desiree did not return to the hotel suite, and Benjamin Faring-Brown had pledged to make arrangements to secure their luggage. It had been thought that a return to the hotel would invite another attack. After more than an hour's waiting, they had left by the back door of the shop. Desiree's sari was folded around her again, and covered her face. Track wore a borrowed raincoat and an ancient and battered gray fedora.

Faring-Brown's 1960s-vintage Hillman-Minx waited behind the shop, and they had driven out to the countryside, to a house at the edge of what appeared to be a bizarre cross between an American suburb and a native village. The house was small but sturdy, and Faring-Brown had told them it was his own house.

He showed them where to find his modest supply of liquor, clean towels if they wished to bathe, and he had left—there were plans to alter after the attack near the mosque.

Faring-Brown's bedroom was small, but the bed was large enough.

As Dan Track walked into the bedroom, two tumblers of gin-and-tonic in his hands, he saw Desiree bent over the bed, tucking in the top sheet. She looked up. "I changed the bedding for us."

Track only nodded, offering her one of the drinks—gin was all Faring-Brown had. Track watched Desiree as she held the tumbler, both her hands folded around it almost as if in prayer, her lips parting slightly to sip it.

Track finished half the glass, then set it on the edge of the dresser. He took her glass from her hands, setting it beside his.

He reached out to her, gently raising the fold of the sari from her hair and letting it fall, then he ran his fingers over her dark hair as he drew her closer to him, cocking her head back. Desiree's lips parted. Track stared into her large blue eyes. As she closed her eyes, the lashes long and dark like a veil, he kissed her eyelids, tasting the salt of a tear.

"I don't want you to go," Desiree whispered.

"I don't want to go, either," Track said into her eyes as he kissed them. "But I have to go."

His eyes drifted to her lips, and his mouth crushed them under his, his hands moving along her back, pressing her body against his, molding it to him. He could feel her sculptured nails as her fingers explored him.

They stood away from each other for an instant, and without saying anything, they moved together toward the bed. Track lifted one end of the sari. Slowly, as he held the edge of the sari, she began to turn, again and again. As she faced him once more, the sari was gone and Track let it fall from his fingers. Her hands reached behind her back, and then she raised her arms and the top, which had left her abdomen bare to his eyes, was gone, her breasts glistening slightly in the light from the bedside lamp.

Her hands moved to her waist, and her skirt dropped to the floor, capturing her ankles and covering her feet.

Track stepped closer to her, his thumbs hooking in the sides of her panties. As he drew them down, Track dropped to his knees, kissing the flesh of her abdomen, feeling her fingers in his hair, kissing lightly at her crotch. She stepped from her underwear, her fingers working open the buttons of his shirt. He helped her get it from his arms and he let it fall to the floor.

Her fingers undid the belt of his trousers now, then the button, the zipper. Then her hands were against him, pushing down his trousers and his undershorts. He kicked away his shoes, stepping out of his clothes.

Desiree slipped from the high-heeled sandals she had worn, dropping inches in front of him. She folded her arms around his neck, and Track lifted her in his arms, carrying her to the edge of the bed, setting her on it, sliding down beside her, holding her against him. His lips brushed her nipples and kissed the hollow of her throat as he moved between her thighs.

He felt her hands on him, her back arching, and then he was inside her, her thighs pressed tight against him. His hand was at the small of her back, arching her body up to his.

Desiree's body was molded perfectly, inseparably, to his, and they moved to the same sexual beat until her body shuddered one more time, and his body went rigid then relaxed as he sagged against her, his mouth finding hers, kissing her lips. . . .

DAN TRACK watched the sun rise, sitting on the small low porch in a rattan rocking chair, his shirt open and out of his pants, a Walther P-5 stuffed in the waistband of his trousers and out of sight.

He felt Desiree's hands on his neck. "You really will go," she said, more as a statement of fact than a question. There was no reply necessary, Track thought.

Instead, he told her, "When this is all over, well—"

"I'll be here," she whispered.

"Good," he answered. But the word "when" still bothered him.

BENJAMIN FARING-BROWN arrived after Track had showered quickly and changed into fresh clothes.

The sun was still low on the horizon, and it cast an early-morning glow over Faring-Brown and the three men he had brought with him, men Desiree had said worked for her.

Faring-Brown announced, "We must leave, Major. All is in readiness at the airfield. There is much KGB activity in Delhi. There were inquiries at the hotel and at the field, as well, but my men took care of the latter."

"Really took care of it?"

"In a most decisive way, Major."

"Good," Track told him. All that morning, Track had tried to push the thought that Sergei Baslovitch had set the KGB on his trail from his mind. It must have been Scorese. That was a score he'd have to settle privately.

Beside him, he heard Desiree whisper, "Let me go with you. I know the people you will deal with. I can—"

"You can get killed," he told her. "So you don't go. Have these guys get you on a plane to Switzerland—or, better yet, have Zulu come and get you."

"Yes, Zulu can come for me," she said, looking away from him.

He raised her chin, and her eyes rose to meet his. He kissed her hard, as though he was kissing her for the last time.

Track took his flight bag from the porch and started down the three low steps leading to the ground, tossing the bag to Faring-Brown. As he got into the Hillman-Minx, he looked back to Desiree. The wind caught at the folds of her clothes and made the cloth hug her body. He just stared at her.

The Hillman's small engine jolted to life. "Let's roll," Track said to Faring-Brown, and the Minx rumbled ahead....

DESIREE GOTH sat on the small stool beside the telephone and listened to the operator complete the connection. "Zulu?"

"Miss Desiree, I was becoming—"

"I'm all right, Zulu. Get what things you think we'll both need for a prolonged excursion into cold, mountainous terrain. But bring along suitable clothing for a large city environment. There's a very cosmopolitan city near where we're going, and being able to look like one of the residents might be some advantage."

"I would discourage this, Miss Desiree."

"Whether he believes it or not, Dan will have a better chance with me there. You don't have to come."

"I haven't abandoned you, yet. I'll be with you tomorrow."

"Zulu, you are—"

"I know what I am, Miss Desiree."

"Yes, thank you, Zulu."

"As always, Miss Desiree."

"I'll see you tomorrow, then." She set the receiver down, breaking the connection, and stood. She walked to the open front door that led to the porch, where the three men who worked for Faring-Brown were waiting for her. "I wish a safe but comfortable hiding place while I await the arrival of Zulu sometime tomorrow. One of you make arrangements to watch for him at the airport."

"I shall do that, miss," one of the men volunteered.

"The home of my sister," another of the men volunteered, his hat held in his hands. "It is a humble home, but Miss Desiree would be safe there."

"I'll go there, then, and I am indebted to you for your kindness," she told him.

But she looked at him no longer, staring instead down the road along which the car carrying Dan Track had vanished more than an hour ago.

25

"Do you still have men at the airfield?"

"One only, Major. I felt the thing would be better served bringing the other three to guard Miss Desiree."

"Agreed," Track told Benjamin Faring-Brown.

Track could see the airfield in the far distance—a rural airport like those in many parts of the world, probably with a dirt runway.

As he turned to say something to Benjamin Faring-Brown, his eyes caught something in the Hillman's rearview mirror.

He turned fully around in the seat and stared at the approaching form of a black Mercedes. "There normally any traffic around here?" he asked.

"Very little, Major."

"What about a black Mercedes?"

"I should not think."

"Speed this thing up a little—let's see if he matches us."

"Yes, Major." The Hillman seemed to tremble slightly around them as Track watched through the rear window. The Mercedes seemed to drop back for a moment, but was soon with them again.

"Give it all she's got, Benny."

"I have done that already, Major."

Track glanced at the speedometer. In miles per hour it translated to roughly seventy.

"That plane been preflighted at all?"

"What is preflighting, Major? Ah, the preparations for flying the aircraft—"

"Yeah, well, I guess we can kiss off a fast getaway."

"Can we not just drive quickly to the airplane? Perhaps I shoot at them for a little while as you start the engines and then we take off into the sky and—"

"All that's great except the taking-off part. If the engines aren't warmed up so we can get full power, we'll just taxi around a lot until we crash into something."

"My incompetence. I am desolate."

Track just looked at Faring-Brown. "Desiree own a piece of this airfield?"

"Miss Desiree owns the entire airfield. Miss Desiree owns the plane. Miss Desiree owns this car."

"What else does Miss Desiree own out at the airfield? Come on man, think!"

The Mercedes could have overtaken them easily, but for some reason it was hanging back. That likely meant the man on guard at the airport was dead or wishing he was and that more of the KGB people were waiting there for them.

"Come on, is there anything stored out at the airport that—"

"Wait—wait, Major! There is a recently acquired consignment about to be transhipped—"

"Stolen?"

"Yes, but the persons who possessed it were most negative types."

"And what's in the consignment?"

"It is very old, Major—acquired after the previous owners had recovered it during the Arab-Israeli War. And there is no ammunition for it."

"What is it? A tank?"

"A Soviet BMP Infantry Combat Vehicle."

"It wouldn't be gassed up, would it?"

"Of course, Major! Miss Desiree is very strict that any mechanized equipment be thoroughly road tested prior to sale in order that our customers remain wholly satisfied with our integrity and our honesty and—"

"Tanks were never my favorite thing. What's she weigh?"

"It is not a tank in the strict sense of the word, Major."

"What does this thing that isn't a tank weigh?" The Mercedes was closing in now. Track looked forward—the airfield was dead ahead. Two more cars, a Citroën and a Jaguar sedan, were crossing from the field onto the roadway.

"It's empty weight is 11.32 tons, length twenty-two feet and two inches, width nine feet and nine inches, Major. It is equipped with a V-6 in-line water-cooled diesel capable of generating 280 horsepower and the actual mileage is very low."

"I know, a little old lady only drove it on Sundays. How fast will she go?"

"Thirty-four miles per hour on land, approximately twenty-five miles per hour in deep snow and—"

"I don't need to know how fast the thing'll go in water. You see any water around here?"

"Actually, Major, only a short distance beyond the airfield."

"Where is it?"

"In the far hangar at the end of the field," Faring-Brown said, motioning to the right with his hand.

"Drive us there," Track said as he reached under his bomber jacket, his fist closing on the butt of the Walther P-5. The Jaguar and the Citroën, both cars black like the Mercedes behind them, effectively blocked the roadway, forming a wedge, the point of the wedge toward the Hillman. "Can this thing handle it off road?"

"I do not know, Major."

"Let's find out, Benny. Cut the wheel right—now," and Track braced himself as the Hillman turned off across the oncoming lane, then lurched and bounced onto the shoulder.

"I am afraid this vehicle—"

"I used to own one—you'd be surprised what it can do. Give it all the gas you got!"

Gunfire came from the Citroën, a subgun, but the subgunner spraying was firing too fast and they were in no danger. Track steadied the Walther as best he could, trying to time the up-and-down motion as the vehicle left the road. He fired once, then again, then twice more, and the subgunner pulled back.

Track looked ahead. No fence surrounded the airfield, but there was a drainage ditch.

"We are trapped, Major!" Faring-Brown shouted.

"Out of the car," Track ordered as the Hillman bounced to a bone-jarring stop. Track reached over into the back seat and grabbed the flight bag containing all the spare mags for the Walther and his extra clothing. He threw open the door of the Minx and broke into a dead run, shouting, "Come on, Benny! Hustle!"

Track took the ditch in a flying leap, almost losing his footing on some soft earth as he landed.

Looking back, he saw Faring-Brown start to jump the ditch before he could warn him—but the smaller, lighter man cleared the ditch with seeming ease, running ahead.

Track shook his head once. "I didn't think you

had it in you, Benny!'' he said as he gripped the flight bag and threw himself into a dead run.

Track glanced over his shoulder. What he saw, he didn't like. The Mercedes was closing in, the Jaguar was already on the field and the Citroën was reversing off the roadway.

Track dropped the flight bag and turned, bringing the Walther into both hands. He pumped the trigger four times at the windshield of the Jaguar, and the British cat swerved to Track's left, spinning out, skidding to a stop.

With no time to change magazines, Track grabbed his flight bag and ran after Faring-Brown.

Ahead, he could see the large double doors of the hangar. Faring-Brown was almost up to them now. Running like an Olympic medalist, he passed through the doors. Track ran after him, wondering if he was ever going to see the inside of the hangar, let alone Russia.

He sagged against the hangar doors, dropping the flight bag again, dumping the empty magazine from the P-5, ramming another one home, letting the slide run forward. The Jaguar, a section of windshield on the driver's side shot out, was closing in again, the Citroën right beside it. The Mercedes followed, fifty feet behind. A subgun was poking from the window of the Citroën.

Track grabbed his case and ran for his life, the hangar doors pinging as submachine gun slugs slammed against them, lacing a pattern along the corrugated metal of the building as Track ran ahead.

Track rounded the corner of the hangar. Benny was nowhere to be seen. Then suddenly from the side door, "I have started the engine, Major!"

Track threw himself into a dead run again, toward the hangar's side door.

Track lurched inside, breathless. He looked at Benny Faring-Brown climbing into the BMP. The vehicle was massive, almost beautiful, Track thought. "Where the hell you learn to run like that, Benny?"

"I was the star in track and field at the university in Calcutta in my senior year, Major. I suggest we hurry."

"Right." Track ran toward the BMP, climbing up to the hatch. "I thought you said it wasn't armed."

"It's a reconnaissance version, modified after the Arab-Israeli war, equipped only with a 7.62mm machine gun—but unfortunately we are currently out of stock on such ammunition."

"No sweat, Benny," said Track as he slipped down the hatch. "You know how to drive this thing?"

"Unfortunately, no, Major."

"Me neither. We'll just have to experiment." Track slipped behind what he hoped were the main drive controls, already feeling confined. As he glanced around him he decided it was designed for a crew of three. He shrugged—two would have to do. He found what he thought was the transmission—he could speak Russian but couldn't read it.

"I believe that is a parking brake, Major," Faring-Brown began.

"Right." Track found the release and worked it. He moved the stick into what he thought was first, but the sudden rearward motion of the tank made Faring-Brown slip as he sealed the hatch. "You all right?" Track asked.

"It's okay. I've got another leg."

"Strap yourself in," Track said, giving Faring-Brown a grin, then he checked the periscope and crossed his fingers as he made another stab at finding first gear.

The BMP began to lurch forward, and Track gave it more gas. The doors of the hangar were less than twenty feet ahead, and he would have to punch through them. "Hold on, Benny!" he shouted.

Involuntarily Track closed his eyes and turned his face away from the ocular lens of the periscope. He felt the shudder as the sound of metal tearing metal reached his ears.

Opening his eyes he saw daylight through the scope, and he worked the transmission again into the highest forward gear. The vehicle lurched ahead as he stomped on the accelerator.

He saw the Jaguar ahead, with subgunners hanging from the open doors. Faintly he could hear the pinging sounds as the rounds bounced off the hull of the BMP. Track drove straight for the Jag, able to see fear in the face of one of the gunners as the man jumped clear. There was a sudden halt of motion, and then the BMP lurched upward and Track could see nothing but sky for a moment. There was a violent crunching sound beneath the vehicle, and Track felt his face crease with a smile. "Kiss off one Jaguar," Track shouted to Benny. "How about a Citroën next, Benny?"

"Capital!"

He moved the yoke steering, and the vehicle turned right. He could see the Citroën ahead. "All right! Here we go!" he yelled. More gunfire poured off the BMP, but he didn't care. It sounded as though they were driving through a hailstorm. The Citroën was trying desperately to back up as the subgunners ran from it. One of the gunners was a hero—he was running toward the BMP. Track cut the vehicle in a sharp left and the hero vanished from view. Track felt almost nothing in the handling as he realized the vehicle had crushed the body beneath it.

The Citroën had stopped, and Track grinned. "His engine cut out on him," he shouted to Faring-Brown. "Poor guy—let's go over and help!" Track pushed the accelerator to the floorboard, aiming the BMP dead on for the Citroën. He saw the driver run from the car, then felt the BMP shudder as the Citroën vanished beneath it, the periscope tilting skyward, then down.

The survivors of the Jaguar and the Citroën were running for the black Mercedes, and Track brought the BMP to a halt, waiting.

The Mercedes was already reversing, some of the subgunners clinging to the window frames, scrambling inside as the big car roared away.

Track could hear the sounds of the hatch opening.

He turned to look at the hatch as Faring-Brown stuck his head out, hearing the younger man shout back, "They've given up!"

Track let his hands fall from the control yoke and he closed his eyes. "Only until the next round, Benny, only until then," he said quietly.

He opened his eyes, moving the periscope. At the far end of the field he could see the plane. A twin-engine Beechcraft. It would have to be checked for sabotage, preflighted—quickly, before their day-trippers returned. And then there would be the flight into Pakistan.

In his mind, Track could hear the sound of the bell for the next round to begin.

Bonus! An exciting excerpt from the next Dan Track adventure.

TRACK

#6: Certain Blood

There had been an ice storm in the evening, and now Dan Track could hear the tree branches tinkling above his head like a glass wind chime in the stiff cool breeze. But thc sun was warm, and by midday most of the ice would be gone. It had taken longer than he had expected to reach the area outside Khorog. In the distance, Track could see the Chinese house.

As Track narrowed the gap between himself and Hakim Mohammed's house, where Desiree Goth would be waiting, he thought of what had passed and what was still to come.

Soviet troops had been dogging his path. Rahman Mirza, the man Desiree had chosen to lead him through the Hindu Kush, was dead. But the most difficult part of his mission lay ahead. He had to penetrate the Institute for Psycho-Physical Research near the Russian city of Alma Ata. Once inside, he had to find his sister, Diane, and his brother-in-law, Robert Beegh.

And then he had to play God, perhaps.

Somehow he had to turn around and get out of the Soviet Union, with Diane in tow.

And if all of that could be done, what would he say to his nephew, George Beegh? "Look, son, I had to kill your father because he was a Communist agent. But don't hold it against me, okay?" There would be nothing to say, nothing to do.

TRACK FELT THE HEAT of Desiree's body beneath the sheet that covered their bed in Hakim Mohammed's house.

Desiree snuggled close beside him. The room was cool, good for lovemaking. "I've got a favor to ask," Track said softly. "After I get Diane out of Alma Ata, can you get her out of Afghanistan without my help?"

Her body stiffened slightly against him, and Desiree whispered close to his face, her breath warm against his cheek. "You're going to make the Russians pay for this business, aren't you?"

"Have you added mind reading to your abilities?" He realized after he'd said it that the words sounded very cold.

She sat up beside him, tucking the sheet around her body, under her arms, covering her breasts with it. "Aren't you?" she repeated.

"Yeah, I think I have to," he told her, rolling over on his side, not looking at her.

"You know you won't come back. The Russians won't make the same mistake twice. I'll probably never see you again."

He exhaled heavily. "If I do make it out, I'll head straight for you. Where else would I go?"

"Why are you doing this?" he heard her ask, her voice lifeless.

"It sounds stupid," he replied. "But I figure I have a better chance of doing it than anyone else. I guess somebody has to show those Soviet shits they can't sit back nice and safe and play their goddamn evil games without somebody making them pay. It looks like that someone is me."

Track is Explosive!

What readers are saying about TRACK and Jerry Ahern

Dan Track is one of the best new action heroes to come along in a long time, and he has the best sense of humor of any action-adventure character in print.

—B.C., Muncie, Indiana

The action comes at you from every page. Jerry Ahern is a #1 writer.

—C.B., Southampton, Massachusetts

The Track books keep you wondering—can this really happen?

—C.A., Cincinnati, Ohio

Totally realistic concept. Jerry Ahern's style blows my mind!!!

—A.F., Fort Wayne, Indiana

I chose Track because it is a Gold Eagle book. Thanks for not disappointing me.

—T.G., Glendale, Arizona

Expertly written and detailed, with explosive scenes.

—S.L., Timmonsville, South Carolina